Confronted by the devastation, Drew's first thought was a bomb. But bombs blacken, and his living room was snowy, white with feathers. Every down cushion had been slashed and flung. On the little French chairs, Granny's heavy silk upholstery had been sliced into ribbons. The tables were worse. Wood carefully tended since the eighteenth century had been cruelly and permanently crisscrossed by deep gouges.

A sheet from the memo pad he kept by his phone was propped against a lamp. NEXT IS YOUR GIRL-FRIEND'S FACE, the handwritten note said. . . .

Also by Margaret Logan
Published by Fawcett Books:

DEATHHAMPTON SUMMER

A Killing
in
Venture
Capital

Margaret Logan

FAWCETT CREST • NEW YORK

For Charlie

Chapter 1

It was just before eleven. Morning drinks—coffee, Perrier, orange juice—were available, but a champagne din filled the lobby. In three short years, Libre had become the brightest and most acrobatic star of America's multi-billion-dollar computer software industry. The shareholders, assembled for their annual meeting, were in a celebratory mood.

The setting—the brand-new Omni Space Theater of Boston's Museum of Science—had been carefully chosen. Sales of Galacta, Libre's newest product, were stratospheric and still climbing.

Two men, one clearly senior, waited for coffee. Next to them stood a woman, arrestingly beautiful, wearing pale pink. She kept glancing toward the main door, waiting for someone in particular.

Under normal circumstances, one or the other man would have spoken to Lally, flirted a little. Not this morning, though. Fiscal excitements tend to displace the social, not to say sexual, impulse. Besides, Lally was not quite her usual self. And so, when a tall man with dark blond hair and a much darker beard entered the room, her little gasp went unnoticed.

The senior man had also reacted to the newcomer. "Heeeeeer's Blackstone," he informed his companion. A feeble joke, but the young man knew to laugh. He also knew, as everyone here this morning must know, that Blackstone Associates was the venture capital partnership lucky enough, okay, smart enough, to spot Libre's potential back at the very beginning.

"Andrew Lispenard," the senior man went on. "Old New

1

York family, but he's been in Boston since the Business School. Drew, people call him.''

Drew Lispenard! How many times had the young man heard that name at the B-school? And what was he, thirty-five? At most? A yearning expression softened the young man's features. Others in the lobby, too, seemed magnetized by Drew, eager for a handshake, a few words. Nonetheless, he strode quickly through, looking friendly but catching no one's eye.

''What's the hurry?''

''Not his show.'' The senior man's tone straddled the line between admiration and envy. ''Yet another demonstration of the famous Blackstone modesty.''

''Oh right. 'Entrepreneurs make us rich, not the other way around.' ''

Lally, overhearing everything, almost gagged. It was one of Drew's favorite lines. The way the guy said it, he might as well have fallen to his knees. Licked Drew's shoes. Kissed his ass. Like she had. One too many times. For zero. Zip.

Stop it, she ordered herself. Breathe deep. Slow down.

Okay. Drew had sailed right by without seeing her. So what? He was a man, wasn't he? Men see women with their cocks, not their eyes. A thrill of scorn ran through her. Drew was a man. Nothing more. She'd made a big fat mistake to think he was any different from the rest.

Now what? Walk slowly down the aisle? But what if she had her back to him when he finally spotted her? She'd miss the impact. Better sit a couple of rows behind him. Pick her own moment to strike.

Waiting, giving Drew time to settle himself, she checked out the dozen or so other women present. None of them looked anything like her. The ones with name tags would be Libre staffers—secretaries and gofers, low-level stuff. Then the usual bankers and brokers, fast-trackers in male drag, working the crowd like there was no tomorrow. Were they older than she was? Yes, Lally was pleased to conclude, definitely older. The rest of the women, carefully coiffed and dressed in tactful little knits, must be stockholders. She hated them, though not as much, or with as much jealousy, as she did the fast-trackers.

Lally smoothed her skirt front and felt a shiver of stage fright. Back in the old days, in bed and out, she'd made Drew's jaw drop a couple of times. Nothing like now, though.

A lady stockholder with white hair sent her a sweet smile. Lally scowled back and headed for the theater.

Ben Pokorny, Libre's thirty-one-year-old President, introduced himself, welcomed the audience, and told them what they already knew—that the formal meeting, following the script printed in the proxy statement every stockholder had received in the mail weeks earlier, would be conducted first.

Drew relaxed into his chair and smiled. In many ways, Ben the kid was still Ben the kid. The cowlick. The big grin that could turn goofy. Ben's goofiness, back in Libre's startup days, had spooked every other possible source of capital, much to Blackstone's ultimate advantage. But his voice had changed. It was firmer, deeper, more confident.

"After the formal part," Pokorny went on, "I'll have something to say about our last fiscal year."

Undeterred by the dry, legally sanitized language, someone in the back row let loose a loud whoop of approval. Indulgent laughter rippled through the auditorium.

Waiting for it to subside, Pokorny managed to keep his grin just south of goofy. "I'll also talk about Libre's future prospects, and answer any questions you may have."

The ritualistic introductions of Directors and auditors soon restored normal decorum. The first item of business was the election of the Board. Eight predetermined men, one of them Drew, were named and seconded. The proxy tally had given each Director at least ninety-five percent of the vote. Drew had gotten ninety-eight percent, personally gratifying and a vote of confidence in Blackstone.

Despite these numbers, Pokorny posed the pro forma courtesy question: "Are there any other nominations?"

"I nominate Gloria Steinem."

Lally's acting lessons had finally paid off. Her full, rich voice penetrated every inch of the auditorium. Ranks of male heads—fair, dark, curly, balding—swiveled in unison. Moons,

Lally thought, dumb white moons. One of the moons, two rows in front of her, was Drew. His handsome face gaped at her, his mouth slack with astonishment.

She stood there, tall and beautiful, watching him take her in—first the fact that it really was her, a woman he hadn't laid eyes on for six months or more, then the fact that she was pregnant.

She smoothed her skirt. Looking straight at him, she shrugged, humorous and wry. Everyone who saw knew exactly what was going on. This gorgeous dish was reminding Drew Lispenard where babies come from. Where *his* baby had come from.

At the podium, Pokorny was inhaling some fast advice from Jack Leff, Company Counsel, serving today as Clerk of the Meeting.

"Thank you for your nomination, ma'am," Pokorny then said. "Please state your name and affiliation."

"Louisa M. Baird. I'm a stockholder."

Leff found her name on his list. Then, making sure his mike was off, he told Pokorny, "No sweat, she's only got a hundred shares."

Drew gripped the arms of his chair. His face felt hot. Every cell in his body wanted to vault back there and deal with the brat, the bitch, but he couldn't. Nothing about him mattered, not even that everyone knew he'd knocked her up. Only the meeting mattered. Damage control mattered. Later he'd find out what the fuck was going on, oh man would he find out. But—Jesus!—what's with Ben? Is he *enjoying* this? Doesn't he know that crazy things can happen in these meetings? That proxy votes can be reversed at the last minute?

"Gloria Steinem has been nominated," Pokorny, alight, was announcing. "Is there a second?"

A man about ten feet to Drew's left stood. "Second the motion," he said. Turning, he blandly met Drew's eyes, then sat down again.

Harriman Fraker. The Tapeworm, Drew and his partners called him. Blackstone would invest in a brand-new company and before they could turn around there'd be Fraker, nibbling

4

at some undefended corner of the vulnerable young startup's turf. Twice the man had bought controlling shares of competing companies and started ruinous price wars. In between he did as much damage as he could with stock manipulations.

"Parasitic? Hardly," he'd answered a reporter from *The Wall Street Journal*. "I let Blackstone work for me, that's all. Why should I pay finder's fees when they'll do it for free?"

Fraker and Lally? In collusion?

It was too horrible to contemplate. Drew wrenched his attention back where it belonged. Whatever else, Fraker's entry into the mischief had sobered Pokorny up. Thank God. All well and good for Ben to tear around Libre yelling *Let's have some fun for a change!* The formal part of the annual meeting was no place for creative goofing.

"The nomination of Gloria Steinem has been made and seconded," Pokorny said. "Shareholders present who wish to vote for her may do so now, by raising their hand, even though they've already voted by proxy for the slate previously nominated. In favor?"

One of the older women started to raise her hand. When she saw that no one else besides Lally and Fraker was voting, she pretended she'd only wanted to fix her hair.

"Opposed?"

It had been a very good year. The shareholders wanted more of the same for the future. A forest of hands shot up.

"Are there any other nominations?"

Christ, thought Drew. He's pausing. He's actually pausing.

"If not, the nominations are closed. All those in favor of the motion proposing the original slate will say 'Aye.' Those opposed? The motion is carried. The persons nominated have been duly elected Directors of this company for the ensuing year. The next order of business is approval of an amendment to the Articles of Organization to increase the number of authorized shares of common stock to twenty-five million."

Jack Leff restated this legalese in the form of a motion. A Libre Vice-President seconded it.

"Any discussion?" Pokorny asked.

Drew knew the answer to that one. What if he turned around,

shot her a hairy eyeball? Or would that just challenge her, make it worse?

"When is Libre going to start paying dividends?"

A scattering of groans. Even the people titillated by her first move might be thinking enough was enough, Drew thought. But was that good? Knowing Lally, not necessarily.

"Not in the next fiscal year," Pokorny said. "I'll be talking about R&D, Research and Development, later on."

"I'm not talking R&D. I'm talking dividends."

Pokorny was clipped, but carefully polite. "I'll explain the relationship between the two when we come to that part of the meeting."

Drew glanced around. She had sat down. In parliamentary procedure terms, she'd yielded the floor.

He jumped to his feet. "Mr. Chairman? I move a ten-minute recess."

"Second," barked Leff.

Pokorny looked bewildered.

"Call for a vote," Leff told him. "Fast."

Pokorny did. The ayes had it, and Drew made straight for Lally.

The five men between her and the aisle got out of the way fast, so only the couple just in front got kicked as Drew lifted her high. Once in the aisle she kicked more wildly still. He was afraid he'd drop her, hurt the baby, so he let her legs go, keeping a hard grip on her outside arm and wedging her hipbone above his own.

"Ow. You're bruising me. Good. Evidence. I'll sue. *Ow*."

He eased his grip, though not enough for her to wriggle free. Every third step or so she managed to put a foot on the floor. Otherwise she dangled like a rag doll. A pregnant rag doll. The aisle was perfectly clear. No one stood to block anyone else's view.

"Put me *down*," she yelled, kicking at his powerfully striding legs.

He pushed open the door of the theater. "Wave good-bye," he panted. "No more audience for Lally."

As he'd hoped, she stopped struggling once he got her out to the sidewalk. Miraculously, a cab stopped to discharge a mother and her two kids. Drew pushed Lally into the back seat and climbed in beside her.

The address he gave was Lally's mother's, in Chestnut Hill. As soon as she heard it, Lally started screaming. The driver slammed the speaking port. Driving a cab you met all kinds. But at the Science Museum in the middle of the morning?

Chapter 2

Carrying the roast beef on rye he'd picked up for a desk lunch, Drew was back in the office by twelve-thirty.

A strong smell of raw onion emanated from the Managing Partner's office. Rob Kellner, a thin, intense man with a lab-bench stoop and a Newtonian gleam in his eye, was having a desk lunch too, a sub, crunchy with red pepper flakes. With him was the rest of Blackstone, Sam Pardee.

Sam's bald head shone, indicating exertion and worry. He was rapidly forking salad out of a plastic tub the size of a blockbuster novel. Sam believed that salad, however loaded up with hard-boiled egg, julienned ham, and sludgy blue cheese dressing, was diet food.

News travels fast in Boston's clubby financial community. Drew knew immediately that his partners had heard the worst of the morning's spectacle.

He indicated the paper bag he was carrying. "Everyone's being cheap today. Want more company?"

"Sure," said Rob. "You can tell us what you're going to name the baby."

Involuntarily, Drew glanced toward the open door. Linda, Rob's secretary, was just outside, proofreading a report. Her back looked awfully alert for proofreading.

Rob gave a short laugh. "Shut it if you want. Word's already out, though."

Sometimes Rob acted mad to make people stop stalling and take action. Right now he wasn't acting. Sam wasn't either.

Drew shut the door, telling himself it was to spare the office staff in case there was yelling. Women hate to hear men yell, same as men hate to see women cry.

Speaking calmly and slowly, he told his partners exactly what had happened at the annual meeting. He'd satisfied himself, he added, that Lally didn't know Fraker from Adam. True, Fraker could easily find out who she was, discuss with her some other bright ideas for giving Blackstone a hard time. "But I doubt she'd cooperate. She did what she set out to do. She's not a woman to repeat herself."

Sam looked skeptical. "Women in that condition are totally unpredictable."

Drew didn't want to discuss Lally's condition. Not yet, anyway. "She wanted to hit me where it would hurt. She succeeded. End of story. She doesn't want me back." He risked a small smile. "We broke up almost six months ago, remember."

"Yeah, but the kid."

"Even so."

While his partners were deciding whether or not this was believable, Drew bit into his sandwich.

"Is this the same girl," Sam asked, "who shot up your neighbors?"

"No. That was Maria." Drew lived on Beacon Hill, an area of Boston where the eighteenth and nineteenth century houses back up on charming walled gardens. Drew's neighbors liked to party in their gardens. Maria was a light sleeper. The second time this particular party waked her, she groped around, found her pocketbook, and dug out her little pearl-handled pistol. Casualties were confined to windows, but it made TV and both papers. Maria's father, in best Boston pal o' pol style, had to pull many, many strings. One by one, people decided not to press charges.

Had Maria broken up with him, or the other way around? Drew wasn't sure. In the aftermath of the shooting, things sort of fell apart.

Rob had finished his sub and was folding his onion-strewn wrappings into a neat but bulky packet. "Look at that," he morosely invited. "No wonder the dumps're full. Takeout's smothering us. Burying us alive."

"Money in garbage," Sam observed, not for the first time.

Undeterred by toxic ash and problematic technology, Sam

was still crazy about the concept of turning trash into energy. So far, Drew and Rob had resisted investing any of Blackstone's money in this area. The ears they were holding to the ground told them that control was going to come from the other direction—stringent federal bans on excess packaging and the like.

Had the subject been changed? Could they start talking like venture capitalists again? Drew hoped so. However, it would be a mistake to say anything that assumed this. Because of him, Libre had been upset and Blackstone embarrassed. He had to stay on the carpet until Rob and Sam let him off it. Which Rob, apparently, was not yet ready to do.

"Back to this morning," he now said, raking a couple of new corkscrews into his thick, springy hair. "Your personal life is your own business. That's clear, right? But when it gets in the papers or threatens to bust up an annual meeting, your business becomes Blackstone business. That fellow said it all. What we're selling is good judgment. People shouldn't have cause to question it."

He was talking about Gerry Mortimer. Mortimer, an analyst at Burnes, Strickland, the brokerage giant, had been quoted in the *Herald*'s account of Maria's shootout. God knows what Mortimer might have to say about this latest mess.

"I'm as concerned as you are," said Drew. "It's not going to happen again."

Rob's eyebrows lifted. Drew said nothing. After Maria, he'd made the same promise. And before Maria, there'd been Caren. When Drew broke up with Caren, she started taking his secretary out to lunch at fancy restaurants like Maison Robert. One of the best secretaries he'd ever had, ruined by an ex-girlfriend's vengeful gossip.

Who else? Sukey, with her cans of spray paint. Then Jill. Quite a parade, going all the way back to Julia, his wife for two stormy years. Though you couldn't say the parade had begun with Julia. The parade had begun in North Haven, Maine, with Kitsy Blair. She'd been thirteen, he eleven and a half.

Sam cleared his throat. "The whole idea of partnership is on the line here. These escapades put Rob and me in a terrible position. How're we supposed to make a partner behave himself? We can't fire you. We can't cut your percentage. We're stuck with each other. We *want* to be stuck with each other, for Christ's sake. We're a team. Best team in the business.''

"Right," said Drew. "Absolutely."

Sam sighed. "You shouldn't let things happen that make me wish I was your boss instead of your partner."

Rob couldn't have said that, Drew knew. It was hard hearing it from Sam, but from Rob it would have been worse.

The three men sat in silence. Finally Rob spoke. "I don't say get married again. I simply want to remind you that two of us are married and happy about it. Our wives don't shoot the neighbors. They don't corrupt our office staff. They don't undermine Blackstone's good name. Give it some thought."

"I will."

"AIDS," Sam blurted.

Drew goggled at him.

"I read stuff, I worry. Sorry. Let's drop it right there."

Rob fussed attentively with his pile of pink slips.

Sam wiped his bald head with his handkerchief.

"One last thing," Rob finally said. "The paternity issue. Your business entirely, but if it reads 'heartless' to the folks out there, Blackstone suffers. As soon as you know your intentions, I'd like to hear them."

"A while ago you asked what I was going to call the baby. How's Spalding grab you?"

They didn't get it.

"There isn't any baby. She let some air out of her kid brother's basketball and wrapped it on with adhesive tape. Stuffed everything into a pair of fat-lady pantyhose."

"Jesus Christ." Sam, father of four and the least worldly of the partners, was awestruck.

Rob was furious. "Goddamit, Drew! What are you, jerking us around? You think it's funny?"

Drew had never been more serious. "The people at the Libre meeting didn't know it was a fraud. I wanted to give you guys a chance to play with the same cards everyone else is holding."

Before this could be digested, Rob's phone buzzed. Linda apologized for interrupting, but a man they'd been trying to reach all week was on the line.

11

Before Rob took his call, the three partners achieved a quick meeting of minds. The sooner the world knew about young Spalding, the better. "And remember," Rob warned, "these are perilous days for red-blooded manhood. Keep it light, but watch for inferences."

Sam had a better idea. "How about we hint Drew was a little disappointed?"

"Okay with you, Drew?"

It was. The word *disappointed*, in fact, had suddenly brought into focus a blurry corner of the morning's shenanigans. Lally, even back in the wanton bloom of hot romance, wasn't someone he'd pick to raise children—his or anyone else's. Sitting next to her in that cab, though, believing that the child she was carrying was almost certainly his own, he had not entirely minded being selected, by fate and lust, for fatherhood.

An unexpected idea. Unsettling.

Six months ago, after he and Lally had their parting fight, she'd taken enough pills to need a stomach pump. That had finished him for intense involvements.

Playing the field as he now was, he had hardly any private life worthy of the term—which was why he'd been able to assure Rob and Jim that his craziness with women was history. Lally especially was an unlikely source of future trouble. According to her mother, the Spalding episode had been her way of wiping the slate clean so she could marry the man she'd met immediately after Drew.

Playing the field wasn't so bad. Mainly you had to remember that horniness can't kill. That no one has ever died from horniness.

Lally's overdose, then, had changed his life. If he really did want to be a father, far bigger changes lay ahead. Where to start, though? With the fact that someone like Lally, no mental giant and the princess royal of loony, could pull a man's strings, shape his life?

Baffling, all of it. No wonder he felt agitated.

Chapter 3

The three founders of Blackstone Associates had named their partnership audaciously.

The waterpower of the Blackstone River, running from Massachusetts to Narragansett Bay, had driven America's first mills of the Industrial Age—a beginning that would soon make the young nation rich and powerful. Taking off from this, Blackstone Associates was determined to become no less a driving force in the country's newest and by far most potent burst of economic might, the Electronic Age.

Exposing grand ambition is dangerous, especially in a city as conscious of tradition as Boston. High flyers fall harder in such places. Scorekeepers inclined toward *schadenfreude* have longer memories.

"But what the hell," Drew had said at the partnership's christening. "Audacity's the name of the venture game."

"Low risk, low reward," Rob agreed.

"No pain, no gain," Sam concluded.

Which is not to say they didn't breathe easier after the success of Libre, and easier still after the profitability of subsequent investments proved that Libre was no mere lucky flash in the pan.

It was a fast-paced life, draining if not so reliably sweetened by novelty. Much of the time the partners were out of the office, maintaining Blackstone's visibility in the highly competitive world of East Coast finance, attending board meetings, holding entrepreneurial hands. Friday mornings, however, were sacred, reserved for internal appraisal and plans for the future.

By this particular Friday, the Libre ruckus had begun to fade. Once Drew had satisfied himself that Ben Pokorny didn't consider him a total idiot, he had no trouble taking the kidding that came his way from others. "Bouncing baby boy" figured in ninety-five percent of the jokes. Drew's broker phoned with a merry rigmarole about rubbers, safe sex, and rubber balls.

The most instructive remark came for a man named Nat Partridge. "Girls like that can really do a job on you," Partridge had said with a grave shake of his head. "I know from personal experience."

Nat Partridge, the boy from beneath contempt. A claim of solidarity from someone like that hit Drew hard. He didn't hit back, but he'd wanted to. Minutes later he was ambushed again, this time by the recollection of something his father used to say: "Live your public life as if it were private, your private life as if it were public."

John Lispenard had been dead eighteen years. Strange that his words had leaped from memory so vividly, delivering, for the first time, their full sense and import.

Partridge joining Lally as mentor? Someone was really holding Drew's nose in it.

The three partners, as usual, had gathered around the conference-room table. One of Blackstone's principles was evident in the simple functionality of this room and the rest of the office. Entrepreneurs who have been struggling along in makeshift surroundings shouldn't be slapped in the face with a lot of fancy decor.

That point decided, there were certain concessions. The view of Boston Harbor was one of the best in the city. Chairs were masterpieces of ergonomic design and upholstered in rich greens. The baronial mahogany desks, glass-fronted bookcases, and conference table had symbolic as well as antique value. They had been liberated by a misguided renovation at the engineering firm founded by Sam Pardee's grandfather. The headquarters of Pardee Bros. was on the Blackstone River.

As they did each week, the partners first reviewed the current portfolio—the twenty or so companies that had ceded to Blackstone a say in their destiny and a chunk of their equity in exchange for financial support. There was nothing dry or formulaic about this fiscal, managerial, and marketing review.

Blackstone invested only in startup companies. Young companies usually have young managements. Seasoned judgment being in short supply, trouble could boil up out of nowhere, requiring interventions undreamed of in standard business practice or business-school curriculums.

Present-day reality tamed, feet went up, chairs tipped back. It was time to confront the future—the opportunities for new investment. The country was on an entrepreneurial binge without letup. With so many Americans eager to start their own businesses, every week brought in fresh proposals for consideration. Some were silly, some feasible. A few were downright mouthwatering.

The future was the trio's true element. Before long, the unadorned space around the massive conference table began to hum with possibility, iridescent and boundless.

It tickled Drew. The three of them, for all their hardheaded engineering, scientific, and business training, were incorrigible dreamers. Anything could happen, anything. Among the proposals scattered across the burnished wood might be one from the next Ken Olsen itching to start the next Digital. Drew never forgot that Digital Equipment, a muilti-billion-dollar giant today, had begun life with a tiny $70,000 equity investment from ARD, one of the first venture capital companies in the country. Ten years later, after Digital's initial public offering of stock, that $70,000 was worth over $250 million and climbing fast.

And, Drew would happily remind himself, records are made to be broken. Look at the way H. Ross Perot had parlayed a thousand-dollar startup into a company General Motors paid two and a half billion for.

"Want to begin with this?" he now asked, selecting a folder from the pile in front of him.

"Oh boy," said Sam, recognizing the format. "Another red-hot co-investment from Hammond, Halsey."

Hammond, Halsey was an old-line Boston venture capital firm famous for fiscal caution.

"It's biotech," Drew explained.

The others frowned. Biotech was a world-class tease, a singer of siren songs that had lured many an investment fund to its death. Early on, when the very word *biotech* promised instant magic, Blackstone had been burned. Once was enough, the partners' frowns were saying.

"There's more bad," said Drew. "The deal's being handled by Nat Partridge."

Rob winced. Sam ducked for cover. Neither of them knew, of course, that Partridge had been an agent of Drew's resolve to reform his private life. What they knew was what everyone in Boston finance knew—Nat Partridge was trouble. Also rich with inherited money. Hammond, Halsey had brought him in as a partner during the capital drought of the mid-seventies. It was generally assumed they'd regretted it ever since.

"He's looking for a million dollars."

Sam was genuinely shocked. "The Unguided Missile is dealing in millions? Charlie Hammond's slipped his moorings."

"That's it for bad," said Drew. "Here's the good. The company's called Dynagen. Eight months old. Founders are two doctors—Wade Cantrell and Lawrence Morse. They were key in the research team at Mass. Memorial that isolated the multiple sclerosis viruses."

Sam perked up. "I read about that. It was a viral cluster, right?"

"Right. Morse and Cantrell discovered the linkage system that lifted the lid on the whole nasty package. Dynagen was born while the champagne corks popped. Hammond, Halsey seeded them a half million to rent space and buy equipment. This second financing—a million from Hammond, Halsey, a million from us or someone like us—is to buy everything else. Lab staff, office staff, more space, fancier equipment."

Rob sighed. "Including a Mercedes or two, no doubt."

"Sounds like a research playpen," Sam said. "The kind of setup where you mention profits and everyone faints."

"I think these guys are serious about building a business," Drew said. "If they wanted a playpen they could've stayed at Mass. Memorial."

"Unless there was a problem," said Rob. "A clash of egos. Hotshot scientists are always having clashes of egos."

"Except for one thing," said Drew. "The head of the Mass. Memorial team, a very heavy hitter named Ralli, Dr. Louis Ralli, is on the Dynagen Board of Directors."

Rob was penitent. "I better watch myself. I'm getting to be a suspicious old man."

Sam leafed through the folder to find the Board list. "Is Ralli purely for luster or does he have active input?"

"Active input."

"Impressive. Very impressive. They still working on MS? God, what a horrible disease."

Drew grinned. "They say they're closing in on a miracle cure."

Rob was the first to speak. "Ralli's put his name on that?"

"Uh huh."

"Wait," said Sam. "If Dynagen's as good as it sounds, how did it end up in the lap of the Unguided Missile?"

"The research facility at Mass. Memorial has two trustees. One's Partridge. The other is his sister."

"The grandfather endowed it?"

Drew nodded. Disgusted, Sam skated the folder down the table. He was the partnership's egalitarian. The potency of inherited money or family connections infuriated him.

"Look on the bright side," said Drew. "Nepotism is ruining the republic, but at least it's clear how Partridge got dealt in. Charlie Hammond hasn't slipped his moorings."

Sam thought this over. "I like old Charlie," he finally said.

"Are you saying you like Dynagen?" Rob asked him.

"Maybe not for a million. But enough for a closer look, sure. It's not every day a miracle cure comes down the hopper. And if fuddyduds like Hammond, Halsey are springing for it, can brash young risktakers do less?"

Brash young risktakers was what they'd been called in a recent article in the *New York Times* business section. Sam, who looked like a middle-aged Bavarian brewer, tossed the racy phrase into every conversation that would hold it.

There are many ways to play the venture game. Some groups dispassionately dispense cash, others leverage tax write-offs and paper value. Blackstone prided itself on the tact and skill of its "hands-on" methods. Their marketing and managerial expertise, their network of contacts—these intangibles, the partners were convinced, worked no less powerfully toward a young company's success than the capital funding they provided. Because of this conviction, Blackstone's investment decisions rested heavily on the personalities of the entrepreneurs involved. Inspired technology was important. Inspired management was much more important.

Drew's next step, then, was to meet with the doctors, Morse and Cantrell. Ideally there'd be several meetings, separated by what Blackstone called cooking time. At the end of the process, Drew would know whether the fit was a good one.

After far too much telephone tag, Morse and Cantrell granted Drew an audience. He'd have to be brief. Their place, not his.

Minutes into this encounter, the doctors' message, already clear, was rammed home. They were in the business of developing a miracle cure—the first of many, by all indications. Drew, supposedly, was in the business of financing such endeavors. The advice Blackstone was apparently so proud of and eager to dispense was irrelevant. "I don't want to seem rude," Cantrell said at one point, "but for a financial type to tell Larry or me how to conduct our internal affairs strikes me as the height of presumption. And a waste of everyone's time."

Out of curiosity, Drew tried to reach Dr. Ralli, the Mass. Memorial guru. He was off lecturing in Europe. Given what had happened so far, it didn't seem worth a transatlantic call.

The following Friday, Drew summarized his reasons for turning Dynagen down. "One, Morse hardly spoke. Ducked every single question about the timing of the miracle cure. Two, they'll take our million but we have no say and no Board position. Three, the million isn't negotiable. And four, they acted like a pair of louts whose old man—that's me—wouldn't hand over the car keys. They deserve Nat Partridge. Actually, they make him look good."

The partners moved on immediately to other matters, but Drew found it hard to let go on Morse and Cantrell. They'd *snubbed* him, the arrogant bastards. Treated Blackstone like some schlocky fly-by-night.

Eventually, though, he forgot them—more or less. Then, a few weeks later, Pen Mauran, his cousin and best friend, did something that brought it all back again.

Chapter 4

Drew ranked his friendship with William Penfield Mauran high on the list of life's blessings. Some of their compatibility came from the family tie—Pen and his parents were Drew's closest living relatives. But there was much more to it than family.

Drew had grown up in Manhattan, Pen in Brookline, a leafy suburb stuck like a thorn in Boston's seedy southwest flank. Their mothers had been sisters, and the families spent every big holiday together. Then the car crash orphaned Drew and killed his sister Kent.

Aunt Susan and Uncle Bill, accurately defined by Caroline Lispenard as "the dearest and dullest couple in the world," became Drew's guardians. All three Maurans exerted themselves to comfort Drew's grief and loneliness. Pen, at the time, was Harvard's all-American running back. A god. Drew was a skinny Exeter senior who knew that gods, under normal circumstances, don't bother with kids.

"I can't," he'd say when Pen called with an invitation. I can't profit from death, he meant.

"But man! It's *spring*. Beer! Babes! Rock 'n' roll!"

Miserable, tempted, fearing the onslaught of greater misery and guilt, Drew would insist he had to study.

They both graduated. Drew went to Harvard, gained some weight and muscle, and played varsity soccer. Pen went to Dallas to learn the oil business. A few years later he made a career change, becoming a photographer for the *Morning News*—surprising until you remembered the remarkable sports pictures that had appeared over his name in the *Crimson*, once football season was over for the year.

The dearest and dullest couple in the world were transferred to Minneapolis. They came to Drew's wedding, but there'd been no time for real talk.

Right after Drew's divorce, Pen got an offer from the *Boston Globe*. Drew spotted his byline under a terrific shot of a mallard skidding into a landing in the Public Garden pond. On impulse, he picked up the phone.

The first surprise was that Pen, the god, and Drew were the same size and looked enough alike to be brothers. Twins, if you gave Pen Drew's beard. The second surprise was that they were complete strangers. They did their best, catching up on family news and talking about the three-decker Pen was renovating in Brookline. Drew said a few things about Blackstone and his marriage. Pen was embarrassed that he'd missed the wedding.

"That's okay," Drew said. "You're here for the divorce." But he wondered, once the evening was over, if they'd ever get together again.

What more did they have to say to each other? Nobody's fault. Nobody's fun, either. Almost a year later he gave it another try. Pen had said swimming was good for his football-stressed knees, and Drew had recently joined a club with a pool.

Pen sounded pleased to hear from him. "The Charles River Club? You're going in for bastions of male privilege?"

"It's around the corner from my house," Drew explained. "If the Y had a pool around the corner, I'd go for the Y."

They did their laps, showered, and dressed. Drew had made reservations at the Ritz, within easy strolling distance. Pen's parents had loved the Ritz dining room. They'd often treated Drew to dinner there when he was at Harvard.

"To old times," Drew said.

They touched glasses. Pen, fine earlier, now seemed miles away.

Drew pressed the nostalgia button a little harder. "Your folks were great to me, you know. And you too. All those invitations to party in Cambridge. Too bad I was so hung up."

Pen looked startled. "Hung up?"

"Survivor guilt."

"My God. I never thought of that. Then or now. Wish I had."

"You must've thought I was an ungrateful little snot."

"No."

Something else, then. That was clear. "Let's have it," Drew said, smiling. "You're one of the few people I know who can tell me what I was like in those days."

"Before I get into that, there's something else. Gerry Mortimer—you know him?"

"Not well. Oh, right. We saw him tonight. In the bastion."

"You ever talk business with him?"

"No. Not yet, I should say."

"But you might. There's no particular reason you haven't?"

"Right."

"Well, watch him. He's likely to cause you trouble."

"Yeah? How come?"

Pen scrubbed a hand across his face. "He's gay and he hates it. He'll expect you to use it against him."

"What do you mean, use it against him?"

Now Pen smiled. "Oh. You're broad-minded. The point is, what you are and do doesn't count. Mortimer will fuck things up all on his own. He's probably spreading nasty tales about you right this minute."

"What tales? He doesn't know the first thing about me."

"He'll make it up."

"Can I ask how you know all this?"

"Sure," said Pen. "I'm gay too."

With effort, Drew kept his eyes on the face that so closely resembled his own.

"I thought you knew. I thought that's why you wouldn't come to Cambridge, because you'd seen things in me I was doing my best to keep buried. Not that I was ever a hater on Mortimer's level, but I'm light-years from wearing a 'Kiss Me I'm Gay' tee shirt. One, I don't trust straights enough. And two, I'm basically low profile. Most photographers are, I guess."

Drew couldn't think of a thing to say. He had to say something, so he said that.

"It's okay. Plenty else to talk about. I'm glad I told you,

but I don't expect you to be glad too. And don't look so worried. You wouldn't choose this life. I might not either. Has its moments, though."

The night Dynagen resurfaced, Drew had driven out to Brookline for dinner. Pen was cooking. There'd be another guest, Pen's latest. Generally Drew liked his cousin's friends better than his lovers. This bothered him less after he realized that his own lovers hardly stood up to scrutiny either. A more important difference was that he didn't have friends in the same sense Pen did. Apart from girlfriends, active, potential or ex, his social world was composed of old school ties, business acquaintances, men he played squash with, and his partners.

There was another difference, one that had taken him a while to figure out. It had to do with grievance—what constituted each group's major gripe against society in general. The feelings of persecution or exclusion that Pen's friends struggled with seemed to have a more nourishing effect on the human spirit than whatever impelled, say, a trust funder at the Charles River Club to rail against fare chiselers, government waste, and the like.

The stairs near the top of Pen's triple-decker crunched with plaster dust. Pen had knocked out another wall. Inside was Beirut. "Will your tenants complain when the roof caves in?" Drew asked.

"None of that. It's going to be great."

"Wasn't it great before?"

"Hey. Do I interfere with your pleasures? Come on back to the kitchen. David's here already. Watch that ladder."

David Benoit sat at the round oak table. A few years older than Pen. Medium height. Strong taut body and the kind of French Canadian face you see in old photographs of mill towns—hazel eyes, prominent, fleshy nose, full, rather pursed lips. Light brown hair, a little thin on top. Firm handshake. Calluses.

Not exactly a heartthrob. Hard to imagine passion. But it was always hard for Drew to imagine passion. Straights, as some of Pen's friends liked to proclaim, can't afford to. Or maybe the reason was simpler still: Kitsy Blair had gotten to him first, so powerfully that the alternatives offered later, after lights-out in his Exeter dorm, had to seem a pale imitation.

Pen indicated a nearly empty bottle of wine. "David brought three bottles of this very nice Beaujolais, so there's plenty. Unless you want something else."

Drew said wine was fine. Tasting and discussion passed a few stiff minutes.

"David's in high tech," Pen then said. "Talk shop while I do this stir-fry."

It was always a stir-fry when Drew met the latest. Stir-fries require constant close attention. Pen could turn his back, hide inside the noisy roar of the exhaust fan until the preliminaries were over.

David spoke first. "I'm sort of a late bloomer. Your cousin's the first person I've been serious with."

"Pen's pretty special."

"Don't think I'm fickle, though. I've been at Cavendish almost twenty years."

Cavendish Electronics, a vast company headquartered on Route 128, specialized in high-tech toys for the military.

"Are you an engineer?" Drew asked.

"I was at first. Then I got an MBA in night school and moved to the financial end." He paused as if weighing something. "I just resigned."

"Big step after twenty years."

"The right step. I've accepted a very exciting offer."

Drew congratulated him.

"It's a fairly new company," David went on. "I'll be Chief Financial Officer. The entire finance department is me and a bookkeeper."

"Quite a change from Cavendish."

A tight smile. "I can't tell you how much I'm looking forward to it. No more corporate politicking. No memos or reports unless I generate them myself."

Something going on here, Drew thought. He's not talking about what he's talking about. "Sounds great. For the new company, too. They're lucky to attract such an experienced man."

"I'm the lucky one. How many people get a chance to do well and do good at the same time?"

"Not many." And not, certainly, at Cavendish, rumored to have generated enough weaponry to extinguish the human race ten times over. "Are you free to tell me the name of your new outfit?"

"Oh I think so. It's Dynagen. Matter of fact, Wade Cantrell mentioned you during my final interview."

Ah, thought Drew. Now we're getting down to it.

Pen shut off the fan and asked if anyone was hungry.

"Starving," said Drew. "Getting checked out really gives me an appetite."

"Oops. I think I'll turn the fan back on."

"Don't." David put out a restraining arm. "Your cousin's exactly what you said he was. I feel terrific. Let's eat."

"First I'd like to know what Morse and Cantrell said about me. And Blackstone."

David looked puzzled. "Nothing. They just mentioned you along with some other venture groups. In the context of the second-round financing. Why?"

Because they're assholes, Drew carefully didn't say. And you're a fool to trust them. "Then why were you checking me out?"

Pen sighed. "Why do you think? The docs don't know David's gay. He'd like to keep it that way, at least for a while. When you were mentioned he got worried. I said no sweat, but he wanted to see for himself. Look, this food's getting cold. Let's solve the world's evils on full stomachs."

He set down a steaming platter of broccoli, scallions, shiitake mushrooms, and chunks of chicken.

Nothing more going on here, Drew now saw, than your basic gay paranoia. Not for the first time, he wondered if they required regular doses of it to feel right. At any rate, he was out of it and so was Blackstone.

Was that fresh ginger he was smelling? And garlic? He decided he was hungry after all.

No one in this house would ever hear another word from him on Dynagen. He'd change the subject even if David tempted him with juicy bad news or fresh evidence of Cantrell's arrogance, Morse's loutishness. Or the identity of the investor who'd sprung for that second million.

Which was, come to think, in the public record. Didn't matter. He wouldn't even bother sending a secretary to look it up. For all intents and purposes, Dynagen did not exist.

Dinner over, Drew kept having to swallow yawns. New love is hard on the spectator. And, eerily, David was starting to remind him of Pen's father, dear dull Uncle Bill.

He learned, at considerable length, that Pen and David had met in the Brookline town pool. And there was much reference to the sailboat that David kept in Maine, not far from where Kitsy Blair had revealed to Drew the wonders of the female body. A coincidence he felt too shut out to share. Save it for later, maybe, when love was less new.

As soon as his manners let him, he pleaded an early meeting tomorrow and said goodnight.

Chapter 5

In early April, almost a year after his first meeting with David Benoit, Drew spent the weekend at Stowe, winding up the ski season with some friends from New York. Monday morning he drove back to Boston, visiting three portfolio companies along the way.

The relaxed weekend—interesting how AIDS had widened the range of après-ski options—followed by three distinctively different opportunities for hands-on alertness had zapped him somewhat. He put his car in the garage and headed for the Charles River Club.

After a fast mile in the pool he felt much better. Picking up a beer from the towel steward who ran the rudimentary bar, he headed for his favorite corner of the locker room. The shabby place had a peaceful, timeless quality. The center of the room belonged to the backgammon players and their betting audience. On the senior side, most of these men, their nude or towel-draped bodies showing thin, ropy arms and legs, slack bellies. The scapular curve dominant, as if about to sprout stumpy little wings.

The mismatched vinyl sofas and chairs seemed to have sprouted too. Hard to imagine anyone buying stuff like that on purpose. Or consciously selecting the ugly green that covered the water-splotched ceiling and walls. In Boston, these were infallible signs of old money exclusivity—and infallible reminders to Drew that he'd never be a true Bostonian. Pen had summarized it best: "Your average Texas oilman wouldn't piss in a dump like this."

Charlie Tucker was rolling the dice. Charlie had rowed in

the '48 Olympics. In better weather, he still gave his scull a vigorous workout.

Drew liked Charlie. The mastermind of a high-tech investment fund, he'd taken aggressive positions in every Blackstone company that had gone public.

They were playing doubles. Including the onlookers, Drew identified seven men at or near the top of Boston business.

He smiled to himself. Egalitarian Sam Pardee had given him a hard time when he first joined this club. Drew had insisted his sole motivation was proximity and fitness.

"Any social benefits come my way, I'll turn my back. Ditto business benefits. Presidents, CEOs, Chairmen of the Board—I solemnly swear I'll have nothing to do with any of them."

Sam had hemmed and hawed and eventually conceded Drew might as well be hung for a sheep since he was bound and determined to be hung for a lamb.

A quiet night. When the showers weren't running, you could hear squash balls thumping walls, an occasional tin.

Suddenly the outside door banged open. Nat Partridge came bounding down the circular staircase, making the iron treads ring. Flinging his arms across his chest, Partridge jogged briefly in place, exhaling loud, vigorous *huhs* of cold night air. The round spoiled-boy face that always looked too small for his neck and body began to turn bright red.

Partridge rowed in all weathers. His special winter scull had an icebreaker prow made from an exotic molybdenum alloy. He also wore a wetsuit, but according to Charlie Tucker, what really kept Nat warm was publicity. The lone sculler, he'd been called in a Boston guidebook. Joggers and dog walkers along the Esplanade loved him.

In marked contrast, the members of the Charles River Club either ignored the man or made sly fun of his various bids for attention. Tonight, though, something was up. Before Partridge could finish his entry ritual, the entire backgammon gang rose as one. Presidents and board chairmen fell all over themselves to get Partridge's ear, give him a matey clap on the back.

The club joke suddenly Mr. Popularity? What had happened? Drew listened until he heard enough words and numbers to solve the mystery.

George Finch, a man Drew played squash with, came over. "What's with Nat Partridge? He win the lottery?"

"Sort of," said Drew. "A company of his called Dynagen is about to announce an IPO."

Finch looked blank.

"Initial Public Offering," Drew explained, remembering that Finch was an academic. "Stock. Very big stuff. They've got a cure for multiple sclerosis. A certified miracle cure. Apparently it came over the wire this afternoon. Dynagen's going to be the hottest stock to hit the market since Genentech. Remember Genentech?"

"Vaguely."

"A circus. First IPO in the history of biotech. Everyone wanted a piece of the magic. I remember hearing that the D.C. branch of Burnes, Strickland had customer orders for a hundred thousand shares. They got allotted fifty, hardly enough for one lucky customer. Had to pick a name from a hat."

"So everyone made big money?"

"People who got big allotments made big money. Charlie Tucker and the rest of these guys are hoping Nat can get them a big allotment of Dynagen."

"Gee. I hate to see fine old Boston gentlemen dumping their standards in the service of greed."

Drew's laugh was grim. "Want to offer congratulations?"

"To Nat? You kidding? Look at him."

Partridge seemed dazed. "Give the boy credit," Drew said. "He can't believe this is happening. Me neither."

"You in this game? Allotments and all?"

Drew said no and left it at that. Finch was a good guy, but Drew didn't feel like telling him, or anyone, the rest. It would all come out soon enough. From the numbers he'd been hearing, he'd fucked up royally. Blown Blackstone's chance to turn one million into fifty in less than a year.

Off and on since he'd gotten to know David, Drew had wondered if he'd read Morse and Cantrell wrong. David Benoit was a thoroughly decent man. Thoroughly decent men don't work for scuzz. But these pinpricks of doubt had now become a herd of stampeding elephants. Morse and Cantrell might be superscuzz, the vilest of the vile. For fifty times return on investment, Blackstone could find ways to tolerate the pain.

And never a hint from David that they were so close to the cure and the IPO. Or from Pen, except for some recent complaints that David had been working nights and weekends. Drew bet he had. Give a CFO an IPO and a one-armed paperhanger looks sluggish.

But enough. The tightly interactive world of Boston finance is a watchful and stern master. A man has to do what a man has to do.

He caught Partridge's eye. Thumbs up. Both hands. Peppy and convincing.

Charlie Tucker and the others saw. Partridge, practically reeling, sent back a fluttering salute and a weak smile.

Chapter 6

Drew woke at six the next morning with a jumpy stomach and a slugged feeling at the back of his skull. Finch had suggested dinner at a new place on Boylston. It had been easy to say yes, the alternative being to eat alone and brood over Dynagen. Settled, comfortable, lulled by Finch's stories of strange students and stranger colleagues, he'd also said yes to a second bottle of wine. Left unfinished, but only because they'd switched to brandy.

Moving carefully, Drew went to the kitchen to put on the kettle. By the time he could bear to leave the shower, half had whistled away in steam.

Breakfast was a large glass of milk and two corn muffins, split, buttered, and toasted. The muffins were homemade.

Drew had met the baker at the 7-Eleven, making a delivery. Liking Sally Spellman's looks as much as her muffins, he'd asked her out. They went to the North End where, she said, she wouldn't meet anyone she knew. Over scallopine, she told him she'd be baking until her husband agreed to a divorce and a reasonable settlement. Over zuppa inglese—or what the North End presumed to call zuppa inglese—she told him yes, she'd love to go out with him again except for a couple of things. She was ten, all right, eight years older. The minute her husband saw reason, she was going to take the money and run—to Santa Fe, where she and her sister intended to open a restaurant. Finally, baking was exhausting.

"Going out on dates—that's the last thing I need at this point." Drew asked what was the first thing she needed at this point. "To be in bed with a nice man," she said. "Who smells good and isn't remotely interested in getting in touch with his bisexual impulses.''

They got together every five or six days. Always at her house. She was the easiest and most frankly sexy woman Drew had ever known, but she had two strict rules. He could not spend the night, no matter how late or cold it was. And if he wanted muffins, he could buy them same as everyone else.

This morning's muffins finished, he turned his attention to coffee. Blue Mountain Jamaican, made in a Chemex. Only method he trusted.

Two cups later, he had to face it. His stomach would behave, but he'd be taking the headache to work.

First in, he got first crack at the office newspapers. All three had big stories on the miracle cure. MS-alpha, they'd decided to call it. In laboratory mice, this genetically engineered substance had successfully arrested the linked viruses identified earlier at Mass. Memorial. Human testing, expensive and extensive, would begin once sufficient capital had been raised via an IPO. Concurrent with human testing, Dynagen would be developing a vaccine for the general population. Their goal was to render multiple sclerosis as controllable as polio.

Drew folded up the papers, swung around in his chair and put his feet up. A 707 lifted off Logan, sooty exhaust pluming thickly behind. The harbor, this sunless morning, looked gray and cold, the city sullen.

Hearing the outer door of the office open, he looked at his watch. Eight-thirty, too early for a secretary. Sam was in California, so it had to be Rob.

"IBM turned down Xerox," Rob began, habit's quick hand raking through his hair.

"Proof that stupidity is not necessarily fatal," Drew responded.

Blackstone kept a Little Red Book of wisdom earned the hard way. This brief litany had been an early entry.

"What's the damage?"

"Fifty times investment, for starters," Drew told him.

"More to come, according to the papers. They're working on a vaccine."

"Yeah. I saw the *Times*."

The two men looked at each other. Rob might be thinking about Drew's judgment, remembering that he'd turned Dynagen down right after the sideshow with Lally had demonstrated poor judgment elsewhere. Then again, he might be thinking nothing of the kind.

Drew wanted to clear something up. "There's an oddity here. Dynagen's CFO is a good friend of my cousin's."

"The football player? Small world."

Clearly Rob didn't know either man was gay. Not that he should, particularly. And certainly Drew was under no obligation to tell him. For one thing, it was Pen's and David's private business. Not Drew's story to tell. For another, it was irrelevant, unless you were the kind of man who goes haywire on the subject of homosexuality. Rob didn't seem to be that kind of man. Sam, if anything, less so. But for some reason—paranoia leaking in from the other side, maybe—it had seemed important to note the connection.

"His name's David Benoit. A good man. Personally, anyway. We don't talk shop. I had no idea Dynagen was so close to going public."

"Sure. I understand."

"I've been thinking. If David had been with Dynagen when I met Morse and Cantrell, we might have got on better."

"Yeah, well. Spilt milk. But I've been thinking too. In the future, if one of us takes an instant dislike to a project, that's probably a signal for a second opinion. Let's talk more about it on Friday."

When Drew came back from lunch, Dynagen's preliminary prospectus was on his desk. Across the top was yesterday's date, printed in the red ink that gives these documents their cautionary nickname—red herrings.

The underwriters were Norris, Pitney & Co. and B.F. Jacobson, Lowe. Perfectly sound, both of them. David had chosen well. The anticipated price range, as Drew knew from last night's commotion at the club, was between $22 and $25 per share. Top dollar, especially considering the flakiness of the current market.

THESE SECURITIES INVOLVE AN EXTREMELY HIGH DEGREE OF RISK, Drew read. A somewhat more than standard disclaimer.

The pages describing Dynagen and its business he scanned quickly. David, along with squads of lawyers and the investment bankers, would have gone over every syllable with a fine-tooth comb. The phrase "miracle cure" was nowhere used.

He flipped ahead to the management page. As expected, Dr. Louis Ralli was listed as a Director. There was one other outside Director, Victor Chu.

Drew was impressed. Chu, founder and CEO of Medimex, was a marketing genius. Medimex had made ultrasound and CT scanners household words and was about to do the same with a new diagnostic tool that used nuclear magnetic resonance. No less than cars and cigarettes, miracle cures must be marketed. Getting Chu was a real plum.

Spilt milk, Rob had said. A tidal wave of it.

There were some charts showing how MS-alpha worked and a dozen photomicrographs of viruses in various stages of vitality. These illustrations had been printed in color on eight glossy pages. An expensive job. The risk disclaimer might have required full caps to satisfy some lawyer's worries, but the presentation as a whole radiated full confidence.

The hottest IPO since Genentech. Hotter. Genentech, like other biotech issues that had followed on its coattails, had no product ready for the immediate future. Genentech had sold on hope and promise. Sizzle, not steak, had created the furor Drew had outlined to Finch the night before. Dynagen was something brand new—a biotech issue supported by an actual product. And what a product! A miracle cure for a dreaded disease—sizzle and steak, all in one.

No more stalling. He turned to the list of principal investors. The list that would have included Blackstone if he'd held his nose and handed over the cash.

What he saw on the page brought him to a dead stop. The entire million Dynagen had been shopping for had come from a single private investor, Harriman Fraker.

Drew couldn't take it in. Morse, Cantrell, and the Tapeworm in the same room? But what was Fraker up to? Why the sudden switch from chasing after Blackstone?

It had to be money. Undistracted by Morse and Cantrell's personalities, he'd smelled what Drew had missed—the speedy transformation of a million into fifty.

But what about David? Never complaining about Morse and Cantrell was one thing. But Fraker! How could any normal human being keep his mouth shut on Fraker? Especially given Fraker's record with Blackstone.

What if he'd been dead wrong about David? You lie down with dogs, you get fleas.

And Pen gets fleabitten?

He had to warn Pen! Drew reached for the phone.

But he was being ridiculous. Overreacting. First the miracle cure, then Victor Chu and Fraker. He was going down for the third time, drowning in spilt milk. He'd call David tonight and congratulate him. A personal call, plenty of family feeling. Couldn't happen to a better or more deserving man.

Within ten days of the red herring, Dynagen had become a media event. *"I'll Pay Any Price Vows Millionaire MS Victim"* and *"Mom Offers Self For Guinea Pig"* stories enlivened the tabloids. *Time Magazine* had MS-alpha virtually on the drugstore shelves. *Newsweek* gave it the cover. And Dr. Wade Cantrell went on the Donahue show.

Audience trust in Cantrell was instant and absolute. His clean-cut looks and thick, silver-edged hair were perfect for the camera. His faint southern accent—he was a Virginian—made him sound gentle and caring.

Further underscoring Cantrell's impact was the quartet of MS patients Donahue had invited, each more attractive, witty, and brave than the last.

As George Finch, home with flu that day, later told Drew, "Suddenly the Big C didn't seem so big. With cancer they can cut, they can radiate, they've got chemicals. Cancer comes and goes, but MS is forever. Was forever, I mean. I'm no fool. I called my broker on the spot."

And so did hundreds of thousands more. Newness—the desire to get in on the beginning—had a great deal to do with this. But something quaint, old-fashioned, was operating too.

Cantrell looked exactly like a TV doctor in the aspirin and antacid ads of the early fifties—ads many investors had encountered during their trusting and impressionable youth. And if nine out of ten doctors, the subliminal message ran, prescribe blahblah for fast relief, shouldn't *you* buy Dynagen too?

Chapter 7

Early one Tuesday, several weeks after Cantrell had wowed them on national TV, a young woman named Fernanda West sat in her office at Hammond, Halsey leafing restlessly through a business plan. She was waiting for the plan's author, an inventor named Coleman Boone.

Nanda had joined Hammond, Halsey two months earlier. Her title, for the time being, was Technical Advisor. Once she had learned the ropes of venture capital she'd be promoted to Associate. Partner was way down the road, too far off to seem real—and too weird. Partners with Nat Partridge? How do you get your arms around that one?

She put down Boone's plan and scrubbed her hands together. It would be a mistake to give the inventor of Paladin— she loved the name—an icy handshake on top of everything else. By "everything else" she meant her inexperience in venture capital. Nat was supposed to manage this meeting, not her. Fifteen minutes ago he'd torn off without a word. All his secretary would or could say was that he'd been called to Dynagen.

With Charlie Hammond and Wink Halsey both out of the office, Nanda had no choice but to wing it with Boone and hope for the best. She knew she could talk to him in his own language, but was that enough? Technological brights wouldn't impress him as much as clear demonstrations that Hammond, Halsey knew how to take his fledgling company all the way to the Big Board. And make him rich in the process. Which, assuming efficient production and lead time on the knock-off competition, was a real possibility.

The size of a breadbox—did breadboxes, Nanda wondered,

still exist?—Paladin was the answer to the most anxious prayer of the Electronic Age. If it worked as Boone claimed, computers everywhere could be secured against telephonic invasion. No more raids on classified or confidential information. No more embarrassing heists of multimillion-dollar data bases by fifteen-year-old hackers.

Nanda, in this first meeting with Boone, was supposed to applaud and subtly investigate Paladin's technology. Nat was supposed to convince him to take less than the million and a half his business plan requested. Hammond, Halsey believed that too rapid a shift from rags to riches weakened entrepreneurial zeal. "Douses the fire in the belly," Charlie Hammond always said.

Nanda had problems with this theory—with anything cheapskate. She hoped to postpone money talk until Nat was available.

Would Boone mind it that she was a woman? Nanda didn't think so. Women were so rare in venture capital that the stimulus to form hard attitudes, negative or otherwise, was lacking. And her body, she believed, let her come across more as a tomboy than a capital W woman.

She saw her mother's startled frown. *Computers? You? Whatever for?*

My hands are cold, she informed her mother and any other skeptics who might be listening, because I'm new at this. Not because I'm female.

And what if Nat was here, the way he was supposed to be? What could she really expect from him, the pompous jerk? How much help did he have in him to offer?

There. It was out. She was still so ignorant that a retard like Nat Partridge could teach her something. She took a deep breath, faced the nasty truth squarely, and instantly felt calmer.

"Mr. Boone," her secretary announced.

A block south, at Blackstone, Sam Pardee and Drew had also been focused on Coleman Boone. Blackstone wanted Paladin dearly. Last week, when Boone had come in for his initial meeting, Drew and Sam had tried every ploy in their repertory. Boone, however, hadn't been ready to sign. First he needed to shop around, see who else loved him and how sweet a deal they'd cut to prove it.

"After all these years," Sam complained, "I'm still not sure whether it's better to be the first suitor, the last, or the one in the middle."

Drew thought first was best. "Especially with loners like Boone. He's heard no, can't be done, his whole life long. We were the first to say yes. He'll remember that."

Across the river, in Somerville, David Benoit was waiting for Dynagen's meeting to begin. Even though he'd been the one to call it, to insist upon it, the prospect of battle ahead was stirring negative memories of his Cavendish years.

Which proved once again that you can't escape the past. Not that he needed new proof. Often at the end of a long day he'd think of his boyhood in Coker Falls and how far he'd traveled from that early darkness. A zigzag of joy mixed with terror would slice toward his heart. Later, with Pen, he'd feel it again, all the more fiercely for his delight in their love, his fears for it.

He kept these turbulent feelings to himself, of course. Pen, if he knew them, would turn away in disgust. Pen understood surfaces. He knew the earth's cooled and stable crust, not the wild inferno that raged below.

Nat Partridge stuck his head in the door. "Quite a rush, getting here on time," he said in his arch way. "What's up, anyway?"

"I'm not sure," said David, who had no intention of getting into it one-on-one. "But go ahead, will you? We've got five minutes and I want to finish something here."

As Partridge headed toward the conference room, David slit open the envelope with the Coker Falls postmark and his name and address written in the familiar Palmer method script. If school was just penmanship, she used to say, I'd be the class genius.

Hello again, he read.

Sitting very straight, he finished reading. The letter was short, but when he had refolded it and slid it back inside its envelope, he saw that the full five minutes had elapsed. He would be thirty seconds late. Time enough for Partridge and everyone else to learn who had called the meeting. Time enough for the opposition to consolidate.

His face expressionless, David hurried out of his office and down the hall.

An hour and a half later, back at his desk, he opened the rest of his mail, jotting answers for his secretary's guidance. The phone rang. It was a broker, a man he knew fairly well, from Paine Webber. David answered his questions about the IPO as if nothing had happened. As if the planet hadn't split open with a thunderous roar. As if every last one of them wasn't buried alive under endless heaps of flaming rubble.

When the Paine Webber man hung up, David was shaking uncontrollably, nearly in tears. It was time to leave.

He dialed Phil Spurling, the manager of the boatyard up in Tenants Harbor, Maine. He'd be taking the *Becky T.* out that evening, he told Spurling.

"Tonight? But she's still hauled."

"Then sometime in the next couple of hours you better launch her."

Spurling invariably argued with city people. This time, hearing what edged David's voice, he didn't bother. Foolish as it was to take a sailboat out on a cold April night, it was more foolish still to cross someone as hell-bent as Mr. David Benoit.

Chapter 8

Wednesday morning, when David awoke in the *Becky T.*'s snug cabin, he was astonished to find the sun already high.

He'd slept like a dead man. No regret-pestered tossing and turning, no dreams. Instead, the events of the day before—his flight from the office, the note he'd hastily scribbled to Pen, his stop at L.L. Bean to pick up rations—seemed dreamlike. Particularly unreal was the short sail from Spurling's boatyard to Seal Harbor, where he was now anchored. The cold, quiet night, lit by a bright half moon, was a distant memory.

He had begun more cruises than he could count with this same ghosting reach up the coast, but more than familiarity had gotten him safely here. He had been, he now realized, in a kind of shock. He'd operated on automatic pilot. For proof, the cabin was warm, and he had no recollection of lighting the tricky Aladdin stove.

There was an important lesson about habit in this. He'd come to this clean and simple place to settle himself, to confront chaos and wrestle it to the ground. For the next five days—he'd given himself until Sunday—he would consciously follow habit and do everything as normally as possible.

He started water for his coffee and shook some granola into a bowl.

Across Muscle Ridge Channel, hidden in the lee of a tiny island, Dan Richardson stared balefully at his radar screen and the bright stationary dot that was the *Becky T.* He'd hardly slept for tending the screen, listening in on the VHF. After first light, even dozing was out. He had to catch the first sign of movement.

The sun rose higher. What was this Benoit waiting for? Not tide. No one with any kind of auxiliary waits for tide. Especially city sailors. But then why the fuck wasn't he sailing?

The fisherman's chatter on the box was driving Richardson bananas. Their asshole codes, pretending they were talking baseball instead of schools of fish.

Fish. Deep disgust filled him. The only smart thing about fishermen was how fast they'd gone deaf, dumb, and blind about unusual boat activity. Every last one was scared shitless he'd catch a friend's kid running dope, making money for himself instead of the bank—which was a real break for him on this job here. If he had to, he could hang out all day, as good as totally invisible.

The sharp-toothed animal that lived in his fleshy gut helped itself to a good chaw. Richardson swore without passion. He and his animal went back a long ways together. Running dope, making money, was supposed to have gotten rid of the animal and a couple three other pests besides. It hadn't worked out that way. Richardson had almost forgotten it was supposed to.

David finished his coffee and licked the inside of his cereal bowl clean. The *Becky T.* had no sink, no frills. He'd bought her for speed and her miraculous ability to outpoint other boats.

Last summer on their long cruise, their only real vacation together, Pen had turned the cabin into a garden. A sprout-atorium, he'd called it. Mung beans, alfalfa, and lentils sprouted green and lush for salads. Pen wanted a real cruising boat with a real galley. For the next five days, though, no one could ask for a better craft than the lively, responsive *Becky T.*

David would sail, as usual, for the outside edge of North Haven, or, with a slightly different breeze, the Thorofare. In Merchant's Row he'd make his final outbound decision: Isle au Haut or Eggemoggin Reach.

A wild impatience filled him. Off! He had to be off!

Dan Richardson, hidden in his lee, saw the dot on the screen begin to move. Just before the sailboat left his screen, he turned the key in the ignition. A few minutes later, his animal curled into a cuddy and fell asleep.

*   *   *

Coming home that night, Drew's legs started screaming on the first landing, three flights still to go.

His duplex was at the top of a Brimmer Street Victorian that had been artfully renovated and sliced into condos. The stairs were his distant early warning system. Living sanely, he never noticed them or minded the absence of an elevator. Anything else—a crisis at work, missed meals, pressures met by brandy instead of exercise—turned the climb into a chore.

Tonight it was a chore, made worse by his ringing phone.

"I was about to hang up."

"Hello?"

"It's me, Drew."

"Pen. Sorry. My head's still at the office."

"Can we get together tonight?"

Drew heard trouble. "Sure. But here, okay?"

"I'm pretty loaded."

"So call a cab. We'll eat in."

"Brownie's brown slop?"

Mrs. Brown came twice a week to clean, do laundry, and concoct the mystery meat casseroles that filled Drew's freezer. "Maybe her red slop. We'll decide when you get here."

It had been a day of snowballing frustrations, topped off by Coleman Boone's last-minute refusal to shake hands on their deal. Every venture capitalist in Boston loved him, wanted him. He'd never had so much fun in his life. Blackstone had to give him more time.

The only way to survive such a day is by promising yourself a bottle of good wine and something classic on the VCR. *The Maltese Falcon*, Drew had been thinking. Not until he was under the shower spray did he ask himself why, when his plans for the evening were so limited and specific, he'd picked up the goddamned phone in the first place.

The answer didn't make him feel any better. It might have been Sally, needing a restorative slide between the sheets as much as he did.

Pen was a good drinker except for when he wasn't. It looked like a long night ahead. About as far from a friendly fuck as a man can get.

Chapter 9

"If I had this, I'd keep my windows clean," said Pen.

He'd come in complaining about the weather—the cold rain just starting, the drag-ass lateness of spring. Now, large scotch in hand, he was focusing his irritability on Drew's view.

"I'll mention it to Mrs. Brown."

"M.I.T.'s lit up like Christmas. So many young geniuses— what *can* they be doing?"

"Hatching goodies for Blackstone. Or Dynagen."

Pen drank. "Or the Pentagon war machine."

"Speaking of Mrs. Brown," Drew began.

"I couldn't eat a thing. Not . . . A . . . Thing."

"I'm starving. Red, I think. Lately her reds have been quite good."

"Not a thing."

When Drew came back from putting the casserole in and washing some lettuce for salad, Pen was fiddling with one of the music boxes—inherited, like everything else in the apartment, from Granny Lispenard. Drew showed him how it worked and the sprightly tune tinkled to conclusion, a pair of masked dancers pirouetting on top.

"Cute," said Pen. "Just like *Rules of the Game*. What? You've never seen it? Well, you should. The guy who collects the music boxes reminds me of you. His personality, anyway. The other characters keep saying he's a dying breed.

"Thanks."

"It's on tape. Let's rent it tonight."

"You want to rent a movie, go ahead. I'm going to stay right here and eat my nice red supper."

The bell went off on the microwave. Drew dished himself

out a generous portion and sat down at the kitchen table. "Salad with the meal?" he murmured solicitously. "Please," he answered himself. "Wine? Thanks. Fresh pepper? Just a little."

Pen topped off his scotch and sat down opposite. "Is that my vinaigrette?"

"Yup."

"You've stopped using that horrible bottled stuff?"

"Yup."

"How's that red slop?"

"Good. Want some?"

"Why not? What am I, a tragic hero?"

"You probably guessed," Pen said when they'd finished eating. "David's gone. I came home yesterday and found this."

He handed Drew David's quick scrawl:

Pen—
Gone sailing for a few days—megaproblems. Back Sunday night—explain everything then. Sorry a million million times to leave like this, but it's the only way.
                                        Love,
                                        David

Best to address the positive, Drew decided. "This is the communication of a man who intends to stick around once he comes back."

"You're missing the point. What if something's really wrong? What if he's got real bad head problems? He's been working incredible hours. Something could have snapped."

"I thought you said he was thriving on it. You'd never seen a happier man, you said."

"That was the weekend. I haven't seen him since Sunday night. Anyway, we're talking heavy-duty predictability here. This is not an impulsive character. Two weeks after I met him I could finish his sentences. My other friends can't believe how boring he is. You too, right?"

"People in finance tend to nail life to a spreadsheet. Which isn't without merit. For one, it's orderly. Someone who tears down walls for recreation can use an orderly friend."

"Do me a favor? Don't sell him to me."

"Do me one? Don't ask questions you don't want answered."

"Right. Sorry."

"Let's go back to the note. The note's concrete. 'Mega-problems.' Not between the two of you, I take it."

"It's complicated. We've been talking about living together. His idea more than mine, so he's risking more. With his bosses, too."

"How come?"

"I'm out. He isn't."

"Ah. Moving in equals coming out."

"Of course it does. Have you visited the real world lately?"

"I keep forgetting it's such an issue. And don't bother to tell me that's a luxury reserved for the straight."

"A dying breed. You have to see this movie."

"Are we finished with the megaproblems?"

"Here's how David sees it. He goes on the road for the IPO. Everyone from sea to shining sea sees what a sterling character he is. He *is* a sterling character, you know."

"Yes he is."

"And there are times and places when he's not the least bit predictable. In private. Beyond your ken."

"Happy to take your word for it."

"After he comes back from the road show, he can do what he wants about coming out."

"Sounds reasonable."

"Yeah?"

"I wouldn't bat an eye."

"But you can't speak for Dynagen."

"No. Or anyone in business. It never comes up. Either we're all wearing blinders or they're all in the closet. Like Gerry Mortimer. He was transferred to New York, by the way."

"Transferred? He's dying. AIDS."

"Jesus."

"Yeah. AIDS hysteria bears on all this. Right now's not a great climate for being gay, to put it mildly. What if Cantrell somehow found out about David? Cantrell's a southerner. A Bible Belter. He could've told David no dice on the road show."

"He'd have to be totally, *totally* insane. The IPO is a fiscal event. David's the fiscal manager. He and Morse and Cantrell have to present a united front. It's absolutely vital to the company's credibility."

"Even with the miracle cure?"

"Even if ten randomly selected patients took a spoonful and jumped out of their wheelchairs to tap dance."

"Then I give up. The predictable Benoit has foxed quicksilver Pen Mauran."

Not for the first time, Drew had a distinct sense that Pen was keeping something back. Something he, Drew, was too wiped out to deal with at this hour. "He'll explain on Sunday."

"Right."

"Meantime, how does *The Maltese Falcon* strike you?"

"Compared to *Rules of the Game*?"

"One's here, the other's out there in the rain."

"Good point."

He stretched out on one sofa, Drew on the other. Halfway through Mary Astor's second attempt on Bogart's virtue, Pen fell asleep. Drew watched her third attempt through to their big kiss. Then he shut off the machine, covered his cousin with a quilt, and went to bed.

Tomorrow, first thing in the morning, he'd call Sally.

Chapter 10

By midafternoon Thursday, the wind had slackened and the sky had lost its clarity. Rain, David thought. Fog. The heavy tiredness that had hit him late yesterday was back in force. It's the chill, he told himself. Saps your strength. The possibility that emotional stress was wearing him down he flatly refused to consider.

Probably he should turn in for a quick nap. If serious fog rolled in, he'd need every shred of alertness he could muster. A few miles to starboard, dangling off the tip of North Haven, was Lovelace Island. Just inside Lovelace was a nice little bight with good holding bottom. Bite, Pen had thought it was. He'd visualized giant jaws noshing their way up the coast, chomp, chomp, chomp.

David would anchor there, have a nap, reconsider the weather picture when he woke up. If it looked like his sailing was over for the day, Lovelace was a fine place to spend the night. No people, for one thing.

Yesterday, tired and unable to push for a less populous harbor, he'd had to settle for Hackett's Cove. The locals had been too polite to shout questions, but he could feel their curiosity. At Lovelace, there'd be none of that. More important, the little bight was ideally situated for an easterly blow. He yawned and thought with pleasure of his warm cabin, his sleeping bag, thick with the best goosedown money could buy.

By the time his anchor was set—plenty of scope in case of storm—the wind had backed decisively to the east. Air and water were the same gray, with visibility almost nil. Ducking in here had been the right thing to do.

He'd dropped his main and was about to furl it when he

heard an engine coughing like an emphysemic smoker. Through the gray he watched the approach of a small, new-looking trawler. Its skipper, a beefy guy in a baseball cap, hollered something.

David caught just one word, *radio*. He cupped his hand around his ear and the trawler came laboring closer—too close, David thought but didn't say. Always risky to lecture a Mainer on his seamanship.

"You got a radio?" he now heard.

He shook his head no. The other man swore and appeared unsure what to do next. "My radio's busted," he finally yelled. "First the radio, then the fuel pump. Leastways I think it's the fuel pump. It ain't my boat—I'm delivering her over to Rockland. I was making for the Thorofare and saw you come in here."

David secured a billow of sail. He didn't like this man. The beer belly, the Coors hat, the long, dirty hair—fag-basher written all over him. But the code of the sea was the code of the sea. You had to help distressed vessels.

"I'll take a look at the engine if you want me to. Just let me stow this main."

"I'm obliged," the man said.

Encouraged by this mannerliness, David made quick work of his furling. He then jumped into the *Becky T.*'s pram and rowed the few strokes to the laboring trawler.

The Mainer gave him a hand up. David introduced himself. "Please to meet you. I'm Dan Richardson."

Richardson gestured with a battery lantern at the open hatch. "There she is, the bitch. Here, you'll want the light."

David kneeled and focused the light. "You check the plugs?" he asked. At "plugs" he looked inquiringly upward—to meet, as if helpfully, the heavy stave Richardson swung into his skull.

His body fell forward and caught on the coaming of the engine well. Richardson pulled on a pair of gloves, noosed a line under David's arms, and heaved him onto the deck. Quickly he yanked the arms behind, binding the wrists loosely together with a length of soft rag. Tying the other end of the body line to the trawler's power hoist, he dumped David overboard.

Then he rowed back to the *Becky T.* and retied the pram where it belonged. Aboard, he raised the jib and tried to untie the tack pennant. Finding his gloved fingers too clumsy, he completed this supposedly important detail bare-handed. Gloves back on, he raised the main and the anchor. Cleating down the sheets, he luffed back to his trawler.

Once alongside—earlier he'd set extra bumpers; there'd be no telltale exchanges of paint chips—he climbed back aboard. Grabbing the boom, he swung the *Becky T.* around until her sails filled. Get lost, he muttered, giving the boom a powerful final shove.

Most likely she'd fetch up on Calderwood's, though she could skirt it and hit North Haven just as easy. Didn't make any difference, one way or another.

Almost done. He hoisted the body—if the sucker wasn't dead before he sure was now—until he could cut loose the binding on the wrists. Then he cut the body line, letting David fall to find whatever grave he could.

Digging in his pants pocket, Richardson found the good plugs, made the replacement, and, full throttle, got the hell out.

Once away, he slowed to a prudent speed and settled down for the long haul back to Portland. He was pleased with himself. There'd been that setback on account of the radio— whoever heard of a city sailor without a radio? The way he'd planned it would have been easier—Benoit rows over to pick him up and bam. But it worked out pretty good anyways. Damn good.

The only minus, he'd been out here too many days. Not that it was his fault. What was he supposed to do, put on a show for Seal Harbor? Or Hackett's? But he'd been out long enough to have been missed at home. The word was around that the feds were beefing up their act. If they'd noticed his empty mooring, they'd suspect he'd been out running dope.

The animal in his gut woke up.

He should set his net, Richardson knew. Cover his ass by catching some fish.

A hard spatter of rain hit his windshield. The animal clawed and somersaulted.

The voices of two fishermen crackled over the box. One liked the Red Sox, the other liked Kansas City. Assholes. Fuck the fish, he'd worked hard enough for one day. And fuck you too, he howled—at the stiff, the animal, the feds, the whole-salers, the whole fucking never-ending shitload of grief.

Chapter 11

The first half of Blackstone's Friday meeting was almost over. Drew had been discussing Coleman Boone's reluctance to close the Paladin deal. "I'm assuming simple giddiness. All this courting has gone to his head."

Rob asked who the competition was.

"Daedalus, Mayflower, and Hammond, Halsey, far as I know."

"Say we co-invest. Who do you like?"

"Mayflower's pretty new."

"And Daedalus is a casino. Sam?"

Sam shrugged. "Charlie and Wink are tightwads, but they're honest tightwads. And I hear that Dynagen's made a new man of Nat."

For the second time that morning, Drew reminded himself there was no reason to tell his partners about David's sudden flight.

"Whatever, we've got to keep the lead," said Rob, referring to the only position that would ensure Blackstone a Paladin directorship. "I don't trust anyone but us to keep Boone from bad habits."

Drew knew what he meant. Boone had a knightly streak. Computer invasion is *wrong*. A crime Boone intended to eradicate. Profits, the mechanics of building a business, were way down on his list of priorities.

Sue, their office manager, was on the intercom. "It's about Paladin. Does Drew want to talk to a Fernanda West at Hammond, Halsey?"

"Go ahead," Sam said. "I have to hit the gents anyway."

"Hey," said Rob. "Fernanda West was a student in that

seminar I ran at M.I.T. last year. Not exactly your basic computer nerd. Nanda, she's called. She used to get me talking about venture capital." He smiled. "Watch out for her. She was a very attentive student, and I teach nothing but truth."

Nanda West's voice was pitched pleasantly low. She introduced herself, said she'd been Rob's student, and got right to the point. Boone, yesterday, had acted like a guy with two dates for the same prom. He'd praised Daedalus Capital until Nat Partridge had begun to wish him on that big, busy outfit. "Nat's thinking Paladin will fall between the stools there so we can pick it up. Get a cheaper deal second time around."

"You're working with Nat on this?"

"Yes."

"Well. I'm afraid I think his idea is risky. Boone's got the proprietary advantage now, not forever. He bombs out, it'll take him a while to pick up the pieces. Meantime some other hotshot has grabbed his market."

"Exactly. Nat has agreed that would be a shame."

"Good," he said, meaning good for you, getting him to act like a mensch instead of a tightwad.

"Look, it's sort of precipitous, ringing you up like this, but if we have a package ready, maybe we can head Boone off Daedalus. Nat wants to come in for a half million. You're the lead, and if we need a third investor, we ought to be able to find someone who'll be grateful but passive."

"Sounds fine. But I'm curious. You don't want the lead?"

"Sure, but Boone wants you. Unless he wants Daedalus."

"He's supposed to call me this morning. I'll lay this on him and get back to you." He waited for her to say something. She didn't, so he took the plunge. "Are you free for lunch?"

"Let's see. Yes."

"Boston Proper, over on Exchange? Twelve-thirty?"

"Perfect. Oh, wait. What about Nat?"

For the first time, her crisp professionalism had slipped. She might as well have blurted it: *Can't we keep the silly old fool out of this?*

Tempted to respond directly, Drew decided he'd better play straight. "Fine. Let's have the whole team."

They hung up and the phone rang again. This time it was Coleman Boone.

He found her waiting. Tall, slim, a good firm handshake, good eye contact. "Nat sends his apologies. An earlier commitment."

Drew didn't bother to wipe the pleasure off his face.

She had a nice low giggle. "He said you were large and bearded so you were easy to identify."

Drew smiled some more, thinking how much he liked her thick loose bob of dark brown hair. The whites of her brown eyes were unusually clear. Her teeth, too, were very white. They confirmed each other, these clarities. A new definition of beauty. From today on, any normal face, with normally yellowish teeth or reddened eyes, would look flawed and out of kilter to Drew.

"Hungry?" he asked. "Good. Me too. We're celebrating. Boone called."

"It's on? That's wonderful!"

Drew basked.

"Will you tell me how you did it? The blow-by-blow?"

Women always show an interest in your work. It's their training. Not this time, though. This woman really wanted to know. But wait. She'd be hoping to pick up something useful. Did he have to mind his tongue? Talk to this splendid creature no less circumspectly than he'd talk to any other competitor?

The newness of this, on top of his celebratory mood, made him light-headed. If the headwaiter hadn't come up and saved his life, he'd have said something totally asinine.

In accord with the abstemious lunchtime customs of Boston finance, they had ordered one glass of wine apiece—a Burgundy to go with their beautifully grilled baby lamb chops. A radicchio and endive salad followed.

"I'm almost positive Boone was still undecided when he called this morning," Drew said, winding up his tale. "Your package hooked him as much as anything. All I had to do was play him until he got tired of fighting. What about dessert? Something chocolaty and gooey?"

Tom, the man Nanda had finally managed to break up with, would have ordered fruit, unembellished. What would possessive, cagey Tom make of Drew? What did she herself make of him? He seemed recklessly generous, and not just with compliments like the one about her package. "How about chocolaty and *crunchy*?"

"I know just the thing."

Watching him deal with the waiter, she revised her initial impression that there was too much of him. His lips were full enough and the right color. She hated men in beards whose lips were too red and juicy looking. She also hated it when they were too blond—nakedly hairless and susceptible to sunburn. Judging by the darkness of his beard, Drew wasn't that kind of blond.

"Nat's really busy with Dynagen now," she said as their desserts arrived. "It's great for me because I get to do more on Paladin. Speeds up my learning curve."

Drew itched to level with her on the subject of Partridge. He'd also love to know what was being said about David.

She spooned in some of her almond meringue—it was filled with chocolate mousse and sauced with mocha—and sighed deeply. "Exactly what I wanted."

"A small partnership like yours or mine," he hazarded invitingly, "is bound to get into these overload situations. Dynagen's going to level out soon. In the meantime, Boone thinks you walk on water. He won't miss Nat any more than I will."

She pinked. "Thank you. Thanks for telling me that."

"You're welcome. It must be exciting, unleashing a miracle cure."

"Too exciting. The media are driving us crazy. The 'Today Show' called this morning."

Either she didn't want to discuss David or she didn't know he'd split. "Well, don't worry about Nat. I'll fill him in later."

"Later?"

"At the Charles River."

"Oh. You row too?"

"No. I swim and play squash. But Nat's such a regular I'm bound to see him. How about you? You play squash?"

"No."

"Please don't tell me you stay in perfect trim by lounging in a hammock."

"Oh, I move. Both kinds of skiing. Swimming. Bicycling. I just got a pair of those roller skates with the wheels set in a row."

"Headphones for the skates?"

"What do you think?"

"No headphones. What about tennis?"

She looked him straight in the eye. "I don't play any games that involve scoring."

"Ah. You aren't competitive."

"I'm highly competitive. I can't stand to lose. Makes me throw up, the thought of it."

"So you avoid the subject. Very sensible. Know thyself."

They were both breathing harder than usual, as if they'd been racing. Competing. It was a draw. He hadn't called her a coward. She hadn't accused him of a shallow dependence on the artificial stimulus of scorekeeping.

After squash tonight he was going to Sally's. But that was no reason not to invite Nanda to Finch's. "A friend of mine is throwing a lunch party Sunday. It'll be academics, mostly—he teaches history at B.U. Want to come?"

"Sunday?" Nanda thought quickly. But it wasn't something to think about, was it? "Sounds like fun," she said.

They settled details of time and place. A silence that could be awkward began to build.

I could say it, Nanda realized. It's my problem as much as his.

But Drew got there first. "I mix business and pleasure as much as I can. I admit this represents a new twist. So much the better."

"So much the better."

"Venture capital is supposed to be out on the cutting edge. We're supposed to have a talent for the new."

"Exactly. The uncharted new."

"Besides, anytime either of us feels the need, we can ask for an interval of unmixed business."

"But not vice versa."

She hadn't chucked him under the chin. She hadn't touched him at all. He just felt as if she had.

"That didn't occur to me, but you're absolutely right."

"Since we're on the subject, shouldn't we discuss who'd be a good lawyer for Boone? And there's a small point about equity we might as well clear up before you draft the term sheet."

Drew threw back his head and laughed. But before they finished their coffee, these preliminaries had been nicely settled.

Outside there were patches of blue overhead. Real, as opposed to calendar, spring was forecasted for the weekend.

They shook hands.

Nanda, who'd been considering something, came out with it. "When you speak to Nat tonight, will you—how do I say this? Encourage his involvement?"

"How about the precise opposite. In a way that keeps him from taking offense, of course."

"Is that a possibility?"

"It's certainly worth my best try."

She laughed, her admiration ringing so frankly that a passing banker was stabbed with envy.

Chapter 12

Drew's squash game, this Friday night, was with Phelps Wadsworth, an amiable aristocrat who managed money, mostly his own, somewhere downtown. His real occupations— bon vivant, athlete, sexual rover—were pursued after business hours.

Drew always won their matches, but not easily. Tonight he was one set down and tied in the second.

Wadsworth was about to serve when Billy, one of the stewards, knocked and opened the small door into the court.

"Don't tell me," said Wadsworth. "I'm about to beat this guy for the first time ever and my wife's gone into labor."

"No sir," said Billy. "It's an urgent call for Mr. Lispenard."

"Ha. How much did he slip you?"

When Drew returned, the look on his face stopped Wadsworth's kidding cold. "What's happened, old buddy?"

"A friend's had a serious accident. I've got to go right now."

Drew was about to leave the locker room when Nat Partridge made his usually showy entrance. Hailed by the backgammon players, he simply flipped a jaunty hand, not breaking his stride. Their attention had become his rightful due. Besides, he wanted a word with Drew.

"Fernanda West tells me we had something to celebrate today, so I'm doubly sorry I was tied up."

He doesn't know, Drew realized. David is missing, almost certainly drowned, and he hasn't a clue.

From somewhere, he produced his biggest winner's grin.

"The way I see Paladin, there'll be plenty more to celebrate ahead."

"Oh assuredly. Assuredly. Good Lord, is that the time? My bride will be pacing the floor."

Driving to Brookline, Drew remembered his date with Sally and pulled into a gas station to phone.

"A *friend's* in trouble? Can't it wait?"

"No."

"Aren't I a friend?"

"Most definitely."

"Well, I'm in trouble too. Deep hot trouble."

"I'll call you as soon as I can."

"Drew. I'm in *bed*."

"I'm sorry. I'll call soon."

"Yeah," she said, and hung up hard.

Back in his car, Drew tried to focus on what Pen had told him. The *Becky T.*, with no one aboard, had been found on a ledge off North Haven—a sailing hazard Drew remembered from his own Maine summers. The cops, according to Pen, were convinced David was just another dumb city klutz who didn't know how to handle a boat. They refused to understand that he never, under any circumstances, sailed singlehanded without wearing his safety harness.

"Which was hanging precisely where he puts it whenever he's in a safe anchorage. Proving he had *been* anchored, right? So someone must have *un*anchored him, right? But the cops aren't interested in facts. They're interested in the weather." Anger was stretching Pen's voice tight and high. "They had a big rain yesterday afternoon. A squall line might have come through fast and caught him off balance. *Might* have. Dumb fucks. If the weather was that dangerous, he'd have been wearing his harness."

"Maybe he'll turn up."

"Sure."

"People do. They stumble around for days and then—bingo."

"Are you coming out here or not?"

"Right away," Drew said, hoping Pen would stay mad

until he got there. He shouldn't be alone when the rest of it hit.

Drew tried to hug him. Might as well try to comfort a sack of wet cats.

"Look at this," Pen commanded.

Another note. This one was on ruled paper, with holes for a three-ring notebook. The kind of paper kids use in school.

Hello again, Drew read.

Debbys baby is real sick. He just lays in his crib, he is to weak to cry. Some say its Gods judgement, but I know better and so do you. We know whose to blame. Paul is on the welfare. His boy Joey totaled the pickup. One legs in a cast and one arm and a neck coller. The did'nt have insurance or anything. Cristy is home. They had to take the whole breast. Thats all for now.

Your Freind,
Irene

"I found it in his suit pocket," Pen said.

Wondering how the letter connected to David's drowning, Drew started to read again.

"The suit he wore *Tuesday*."

"Ah."

"I couldn't tell you before. It wasn't my story to tell."

"No." He hated humoring Pen like this, but the man was in no condition for a direct approach.

"Okay. Sit down. It's a long one."

Chapter 13

Pen opened a beer for Drew and poured himself another drink. Then he sat for a moment, drumming his fingers on the kitchen tabletop. "David grew up," he finally began, "in Coker Falls, Maine, west of Augusta. Nowheresville, except that the Cokers built a paper mill there.

"The town and the mill were one and the same. David's father and the rest of them bought food and clothes at the company store and paid with company scrip. The mill owned all the houses. Someone tried to build himself a cabin out of town, away from the sulfur stink. It was torched, presumably by management.

"David's father, Francois, later Frank, started at the mill when he was fifteen. Stacking logs. Hard work for a skinny kid but don't feel sorry for him too fast.

"One day Frank's foot gets crushed. Does he take off sick? No sir. He's right back on the job, bloody footprints wherever he limps. Guess who's a witness?"

"Mr. Coker," said Drew. "He can't help comparing Frank to his own spoiled lazy sons."

"He had daughters, but you've got the idea. Newell, his name was. He takes Frank under his wing. Promotes him. Lectures him on the Coker industrial philosophy. Workers, like children, need an iron hand. Leniency confuses them.

"Before long Frank's managing the mill, cutting corners Newell never dreamed of. One of his ideas was to make excess pulp and sell it to other mills. He'd wait for shortages and when the price was right, he'd drive the workers and the machinery like crazy. Without paying overtime."

Pen stopped and narrowed his eyes at Drew. "Bottom line, right? Good hardheaded business practice?"

"What? Of course not."

"Just checking. Okay. Frank's more than your basic normal greedy pig. He got his real jollies from screwing his fellow sufferers and sucking up to Coker. There's a Chinese expression, dog's leg. Frank was Coker's leg. Otherwise the Benoits lived in a company house no better than the rest. Shopped in the company store same as the other poor slobs."

Pen's expression softened. "The entire time he lived there, David never had a single friend. No one dared pick on him, but no one would be his friend. By high school he was convinced they'd seen into his soul and found fag. He was totally at their mercy. They could expose him at any minute."

Pen was close to tears. Drew kept himself still and ready. Consolation, before Pen had faced the likelihood that David was gone forever, would be dangerous.

A couple of deep ragged breaths and he went on with the story. "David was seventeen when it happened. Paper mills have these digesters—sort of a silo they fill with chemicals and wood chips. Works like a giant pressure cooker. Frank was pushing hard to meet orders. The men had been on two shifts running. Maybe they did something sloppy—that was Coker's case, later. More likely, Frank had skimped one too many times on maintenance, because the digester blew sky high. Hot as lava, wreckage and stink beyond belief. Two men killed outright. Another died later of burns and one, Jack Egan, lived for the rest of his days in a wheelchair."

He tapped the letter lying on the table. "Jack was Irene's father."

"Jesus."

"She quit school to take care of him, such good care he lasted into his seventies. Corporal acts of mercy, Catholics call it. She changed his bags, bought the booze, poured the drinks and mopped up the puke afterwards. It's all in letters like the one you just read. I've seen every one."

"Good God, Pen."

"David started getting them about ten years ago. She'd

write once a month or so. When her father was dying, they came every day."

"I don't get it."

"She writes him everything bad that happens to anyone with a connection to the four victims. Relatives, friends, neighbors—she casts a wide net. And of course he's been worried all along she'd somehow find out he was gay and do something loony with that too."

"But why'd she pick him in the first place?"

"Why not? She couldn't get to Frank. He disappeared right after Coker fired him. She never blames David directly. It's more like, this is terrible news, but I know you'd want to be told."

"Keeping him in the community."

"Funny you said that. I've knocked myself out trying to convince him he no more belongs to Coker Falls than Mars." Pen broke off, his face growing red. "Irene Egan's got to be confronted. You've got to help me confront her."

"I'll help any way I can. You know that."

Pen banged the table with his big fist. "But? Why do I hear *but*? Jesus Christ, who am I talking to, a cop in America's Vacationland? That woman killed David. She *killed* him."

Pitying his cousin from the bottom of his heart, Drew could only stare. Pen stared back until his anger burst into a long wail of sorrow. His head on his arms, he cried.

It went on like this into the night, drinking and angry flailing around followed by breakdown and more drinking. At some point, Drew scrambled eggs and made toast. Pen stuck a fork into his eggs and left it there, fixing Drew with an accusatory eye.

"I know what you're thinking. You're thinking fag fight. An old boyfriend went for David in a jealous rage."

"What I'm thinking is, these eggs taste pretty good. You should try them. Fag's not a word I use, but my understanding is that David didn't have much in the way of old boyfriends. And before you shoot from the hip on that one, I don't think you threw him overboard."

Pen mumbled an apology and ate some eggs to show he meant it. Then, broken record, he went back to his main idea. David could never have drowned the way they said, not unless he'd taken the whole boat down with him, in which case he'd still be attached by the lifeline he constantly and predictably wore. For that harness to be hanging on its hook, he had to have been at anchor. Irene Egan, or someone acting for her, had to have come aboard and killed him, because other than Irene Egan, David didn't have an enemy in the world.

Drew finally convinced Pen to go to bed. Then, exhausted, he rolled himself up in a blanket and spent what was left of the night on the sofa.

In the morning, rubbing his eyes, Pen told Drew something he'd been unable to deal with the night before. The police had said that if David's body was found at all, it might take weeks. "I told the paper my grandmother was dying in Minneapolis, so I can get leave when I need it. Why're you looking at me? I can't tell them about David, can I? Look, forget all that. What should I do about David's mother and brother?"

"Were they close?"

"Hardly. He supported his mother, but they never communicated otherwise. The brother's totally out of touch—in Brazil, last David heard."

"I'd wait."

"Right. What about my own parents?"

The dearest and dullest couple in the world had met David once, last summer. Drew had joined the two couples for dinner at the Ritz. They talked about the weather, Boston drivers, and the weather. The Maurans were "good about" the aspects of their son's life they found incomprehensible, but it was clear that anything personal was strictly off limits. Dearness can't bloom without the personal, so dullness had reigned supreme. Worse, Drew believed his aunt capable of hoping that Pen might settle down with a nice girl now that his special friend was gone.

"If talking to them will help you, call them. Otherwise hold off."

The phone rang. "About time," said Pen.

He didn't get what he'd been waiting for—release from weekend duty at the *Globe*. The rotation was the rotation, especially since the other photographers would be covering for him when his grandmother died.

He slammed down the phone and turned on Drew. "Can you believe this? I mean, it's a newspaper, not a fucking emergency ward."

"Sorry, Pen. I'm not following."

"Not following what? I find the letter. I need the weekend. We've got to get to Irene right away. How do we do that if I'm stuck at the goddamn paper?"

It was as if they'd been paddling down a quiet stream, last night's wild white water safely behind them. Suddenly— *kabloomph*—up surfaces a full-grown whale. Pen's accusations of the Egan woman, Drew now saw, were not simply phantoms of the drunken dark.

Today was Saturday. Drew could leave for Coker Falls right now, spend the night if he had to, be back in the office Monday.

"I could quit. Call back, tell them to take their rotation and shove it. What can they do to me?"

"Nothing. But I was thinking. Two big guys pop in on a middle-aged lady—maybe we'd get more out of her if I went alone."

"And maybe you want me to trot off to my stall like a good little pony."

"You're in limbo. You're trying to balance hope and reality. If you can stand to do anything, work'll help more than whatever else is around."

"Structure. You want me to have structure."

"I want everyone to have structure. I believe in it."

"If I'm at work I won't drink and go on a rampage."

It struck Drew that Pen hadn't baited him like this since David had come into his life. Which was hardly something to bring up now. "Look, if I'm going to Maine, I better shake a leg."

"You're humoring me, right? You're fucking *humoring* me."

"Nope. I'm hooked. You hooked me. One way or another, I've got to look Irene in the eye. See what she's like."

"Andrew Lispenard, ace reporter." Pen charged around some more, swearing the *Globe* would not get one shred of information from him when the story broke. He slammed a new wall with the heel of his hand until it was dented. But the fight was out of him, and before long Drew was able to leave.

Chapter 14

Heading back to Boston, Drew settled how he'd handle Irene Egan. Absolutely straight. Friend of the family. Use the same technique she'd used on David. Terrible news, but I was sure you'd want to be told.

Drew swung onto Storrow Drive, admired the river's dance in the bright sunlight and remembered he'd invited Nanda West to Finch's party. There was a pay phone near the Copley turnoff. She answered right away. Talking fast, he told her he had to leave town on a family emergency and probably couldn't get back by lunchtime Sunday.

"Oh," she said. "I'm sorry."

"By next weekend, things should be clearer. I hope you'll give me a raincheck."

"I think I have to be away. Let's talk again closer to the date."

Drew knew what that meant. "Do you know about David Benoit?"

"I know he's on vacation. Why?"

"He's a good friend of my cousin's. We're pretty sure he's been drowned."

"Oh no."

"Can you meet me for coffee? Cafe Florian's near your end of Marlboro, isn't it? I'll get an outside table."

"Ten minutes."

Drew hung up and punched Finch's number and got a machine. Drew gave it his regrets.

* * *

Nanda was wearing pants that showed her slim hips and long legs, a tattersall shirt and a tweed jacket. Drew thought she looked terrific and said so.

She smiled, then made a face. "Wet hair. I thought, what the hell, let it dry in the sun. Some day, huh?"

"Wonderful day."

"But you've had a time of it, haven't you?"

"My cousin's pretty upset."

"She must be."

"He. Name's Pen Mauran."

"Pen Mauran? Did he play football for Harvard?"

"Hey. They keep score in football. You're allowed to watch stuff like that?"

"I was an innocent child. Didn't know any better. Actually, my brother was on that team. Geoffrey West. No? Geoff would be crushed. I certainly remember Pen. I was madly in love with him. Is he still as gorgeous as ever?"

"I'll have to pass on that. There's a strong family resemblance."

She laughed, then caught herself. "Should we be kidding around or talking about David?"

Drew wanted to pass on this too. More precisely, he wanted to tell her everything, spill his guts. Instead, he gave her an outline—the discovery of the *Becky T.*, the import of the safety harness, Pen's insistence that Irene Egan be confronted.

While he talked, Nanda's mind raced along two separate tracks. One involved Dynagen, the other Drew. The sun on her back, nudging her closer to him, seemed to draw the tracks together. And why not? What old wives' warnings stood in the way? How could any rules about the right way to behave claim as pure and direct an authority as this perfect spring day?

"I know it sounds crazy," Drew finished. "I'm surprised at myself, but wild horses couldn't stop me now."

"I have a friend in Augusta. Cathy Pettit. She's been begging me to visit. How about if I hitch a ride with you?"

"Today?"

Nanda almost flinched, his pleasure was so obvious. It sent her backpedaling into a rigmarole about her professional involvement with Dynagen, her professional need to concern herself with David's fate.

"Fine," said Drew.

"And I'll be close enough to help but not in the way otherwise."

"Fine." Drier this time.

Nanda decided to shut up and went inside to call Cathy, catching her just before she left the house on a round of Saturday errands.

A good friend since college, Cathy immediately and cheerfully understood her role. She would provide the breathing space brand-new romances require. Respectability too, if that's want Nanda had in mind.

"All set," Nanda told Drew. "The HoJo is better than the Holiday Inn, apparently."

Drew's eyebrows climbed.

"For you, I meant." She said it too emphatically, making everything worse.

He didn't leer, give him that. "HoJo's it is."

Nanda couldn't think of a single snappy comeback. The sun was almost tropical. Passersby carried daffodils, tulips, sprays of forsythia. A beautiful boy wearing forties clothes rollerskated past, warbling "Caro mio ben"—a song Nanda, when feeling romantic, often sang in the shower.

The whole city was coaxing her to let go and happily take whatever this wonderful man might offer.

Which was impossible. Not before Paladin was settled anyway. It was just too risky. How can you put yourself in the hands of a man and then stand your ground at the negotiating table?

It had been fun, claiming a sophisticated zest for new kinds of relationships. Now what? Did she have to deliver? Come across? Put out?

Drew was asking how long she needed to pack.

"Five minutes."

"Impressive."

"Maine's the simple life."

"I wouldn't call this a simple trip, though."

"No."

"Remember when I said that I try to mix business and pleasure as much as I can, and you said you were all for the uncharted new? Well, things are getting pretty uncharted here. First the shocker of David and now this Egan weirdness. And you dropping everything to help me out, that's new too. Incredibly new."

Behind her sunglasses, Nanda blinked at a sudden prickle of tears. He was a man in need of simple human kindness and what had she done? Gone all murky and complicated on him.

Remember this, she instructed herself. Remember this exact moment.

Chapter 15

Cathy Pettit lived in a shabby subdivision built to house the planners and spenders of federal programs now defunct. "Not many of us are left on the public payroll," she told Nanda and Drew. "Which is why the neighborhood doesn't look so good. But that's Monday to Friday talk, not for weekends. Specially not with big-time capitalists visiting."

They were sitting around Cathy's cluttered kitchen table waiting for tea. Afterwards Nanda—she had decided this on the way up—would accompany Drew to Coker Falls.

Visit ME, the mugs said. ME, today, was sunny but chilly. Cathy's wood stove was unlit. A matter of principle, Drew was sure. The icy chrome edge of a thrift-shop dinette chair bit through his corduroys. One concession: Cathy had filled their mugs with boiling water to warm them for the tea.

She lifted a fat red calico cozy to give the teapot's spout an appraising sniff. "Perfect," she announced.

Replacing the cozy before any more bergamot-scented steam escaped, she rose and emptied the mugs over the unwashed dishes that filled the sink.

The small yellow plastic strainer had a nylon mesh. "Taiwan. Eleven cents. Biggest bargain in housewares today. Never let metal touch tea."

They stirred in their honey with china spoons.

The first sip duly savored, Cathy wanted to know what had brought Drew to Maine. "Nanda said business in Coker Falls. I hope you're planning to build a high tech industrial park."

"I wish I were."

"I'm told that if you want to see cutbacks, that's the place. We had a terrible case there, just recently. Child abuse. We

69

screwed up as bad as bureaucrats can. All the proper reports filed and nothing got done. The little girl is still in a coma. Dallas Fournier. God, the names people give their children.''

"A friend of mine who grew up in Coker Falls died in an accident,'' said Drew. ''He'd kept in touch with a woman who still lives there. I wanted to tell her personally.''

Cathy said she was sorry to hear about Drew's friend. She'd been dealing with some heavy feelings herself. A woman she knew had been out jogging and a drunk side-swiped her. ''Makes you feel so vulnerable, someone your own age dying.''

They drank their tea and considered their mortality until Drew said it was time to go.

Once in the car, Nanda said she had to talk about something besides death.

"Please do.''

"Let's discuss your car. The suave excellence of this leather. Has anyone ever had the nerve to smoke in this car? I didn't think so.''

"It was my mother's. I don't see myself with a new Mercedes, but this one's pretty harmless.''

"Oh, terribly harmless. Stodgy. Why'd your mother give it up?''

"She wrote children's books. She wanted to write about a sports car, so she bought a Ferrari.''

Nanda was thunderstruck. *"The Ninnys Put the Top Down.* Caroline Kent's your *mother*? I can't believe it. I was *raised* on the Ninny books.''

"Me too.''

"Oh but wait. The Ferrari—''

Death again. ''The bad part was over a long time ago,'' Drew said. ''It's nice for me, having the Ninnys. Knowing other people won't forget my family because of the books.''

"When my brother Geoff told me there weren't going to be any more I socked him as hard as I could.''

Drew laughed.

Nanda couldn't get over it. ''Everyone I've ever cared about was raised on the Ninny books.''

"Me too."

After a beat, she heard what they'd just said to each other.

Drew saw her pink and wanted to kiss her. Where to stop? The road was narrow, no shoulders.

She sniffed the air. "You smell what I smell?"

Paper mill. Unmistakably.

"Let's cut the chat," said Drew, using one of Vinnie Ninny's calls to action. Vinnie was the father. Ginny, Minnie, and Winnie were his daughters. The mother was Mother. Caroline's explanation was that someone had to have a lick of sense and it might as well be the mother.

"And doff our thinking caps," said Nanda, finishing Vinnie's line. "Remember when he was Vincent and the girls spent an entire book trying to come up with a good nickname for him? God, that mill stinks. How can they stand it?"

"They can't. It drives them to violence."

"I just thought—was Pen raised on the Ninnys?"

"Of course."

"Suddenly I have much more confidence in this whole enterprise."

Coker Falls clustered along the Coontacook River. Drew crossed a rail spur and soon came to the mill.

Its grim history and the rotten-egg smell had prepared them for squalor, but the substantial brick buildings were in fact quite handsome. "That tall middle section," Drew told Nanda, "must be the digester. See how it's newer than the rest?"

They drove slowly past the log depot where Frank Benoit, so many years before, had bloodied his foot. A left turn produced a short street of small clapboard houses. This led them to a marked intersection.

"Spruce," they read in unison. Irene Egan's street. Without knowing it, they'd just passed her house.

"Want to go back?"

"Let's see the town first."

High Street was mostly brick row houses—the ones Newell Coker's workers had rented. Some of the window frames and doors could have used a paint job, but granite sills and lintels showed that care had gone into their construction.

"On Beacon Hill," Nanda said, "they'd go for eight hundred thou apiece."

"Georgian. Everyone loves Georgian."

"The evil mill owner had good taste."

"I gather the evil came later. Anyway, Irene's our villain, not the Cokers."

"I keep forgetting. The smell, I guess. The nose has its reasons."

There was a cramped, dark grocery, a drugstore bristling with Coca-Cola signs, a nondescript post office, a hardware store that blared AUBUCHON in shiny green and orange. Another set of workers' houses brought them back to the railroad spur.

"Eight Spruce?" Drew asked.

"Ready when you are."

Chapter 16

The house had been built gable end to the street. A low chain-link fence surrounded the tiny scraped lawn. The first floor probably had one bedroom, convenient for Jack Egan while he was alive. Irene would have slept upstairs, and maybe still did. The bright blue trim looked recently painted.

"Vinyl siding," said Nanda. "Cover-up material."

They tried the doorbell. No answer. The garage doors were open, suggesting a short errand, possibly to the shopping center they'd passed on the highway.

The slice of living room visible from the front stoop revealed a wall of shelves, a large television console and a chintz chair with wide wooden arms. "Look how clean," said Nanda. "Not a speck."

"Look at the *dogs*."

Crowded onto the shelves, they sat, lay, scampered, proffered a paw. They rolled over and sat up to beg in ceramic, glass, wood, metal, plastic, and terra cotta. An astonishing variety of breeds was represented. One, a mutt, lifted a ceramic leg at a red ceramic hydrant.

Nanda shivered. "Let's wait in the car."

Within minutes, an early sixties Plymouth sedan, gleaming with wax, came up the street and turned into the driveway.

Irene Egan was stocky and so short that her plastic grocery tote threatened to brush the ground. She wore a white blouse buttoned to the chin, a long, loose brown cardigan, and brown and white checked slacks. "Machine washable drip-dry," Nanda whispered. "Old-lady clothes, old-lady shoes. Hair's wrong, though."

To go with the clothes, her hair should be blue rinsed and

tightly permed. Instead it curled free, as young and healthy as Nanda's own. Full of copper lights, it seemed to belong to another person altogether.

"Would you like to skip this?" Drew asked. "Wait in the car?"

Nanda's chin shot up in the way he'd begun to recognize. "Certainly not."

When Drew rang the bell, the door was opened so quickly they thought she must have been waiting on its other side.

"Miss Egan? I'm Drew Lispenard and this is Nanda West. We're here because—"

"I know, I know. I saw you parked there with your Massachusetts plates and I said to myself, there's two more, better get the perishables in the fridge before they come knocking. Well, come in and sit down. Not there, that's my chair. Take the davenport. Now you're not going to get anything new out of me, just how I found her and all. Same thing I told the newspapers and the TV."

She thought they'd come because of the battered child. As reporters? Social workers? Thrill seekers? It didn't matter. She had her story to tell, and they constituted a fresh audience.

The hands Irene clasped over the mound of her belly were red and chapped. From scrubbing, Nanda thought. Voice and eyes were animated, face and body doughy, placid.

"People don't like it that I went on the TV. They say I talked too much. What I say is, they didn't talk enough. You can't tell me the Fourniers' neighbors didn't hear Dallas crying. If they'd spoken up, she'd be playing out in the fresh air and sunshine this very minute."

She shook her head as if at some fond memory. "You'd think Dallas *didn't* have a home, the way she stayed outdoors morning, noon, and night. Her little arms and legs blue with cold because her parents—"

The longer this goes on, Nanda decided, the worse it'll be. "Miss Egan? Miss Egan, excuse me, but I just have to ask about your dogs. It's an incredible collection. So many different kinds."

"I have one or more of every breed known. Including Heinz."

"Amazing. How long have you been collecting them?"

The perfunctory question struck something. Irene sucked in her lower lip, shifted her eyes around. "'Long enough.'"

"You must travel a lot," said Drew.

"Why do you say that? I never travel. Why should I? Everything I need is right here, thank you very much."

"Drew only meant you traveled to find the dogs," Nanda soothed. "You know, stopping at little shops here and there."

"I don't *shop* for them. I write away and they write me back. The big places send catalogs. I have nothing against catalogs, but I prefer to have a pen pal relationship before someone starts showing me their wares. Mind you, none of my pen pals think I have a million dollars to spend on my collection. They know I'm just an ordinary woman living in a small town, but they could care less. Nice as pie, each and every one of them. It's funny, you know. When they said I should take up a hobby, I never thought it would work out this way. I never thought I'd have friends all over the country.''

Nanda asked how many dogs there were.

"Guess."

"Four hundred?"

"Five hundred and six."

"So each year you add, what? Twenty new ones?"

Again the indrawn lower lip, the evasive eyes. "I average two per month."

Two times twelve into five hundred is twenty years, Drew figured. "They" must have urged her toward a hobby soon after the explosion. A decade later she'd added a new kind of pen pal, David.

Nanda got up to study the dogs more closely, Irene providing commentary from her chair. "That brown and white springer spaniel, front and center, was my very first. The top shelves are dogs doing doggy things. The rest is human things." A poodle in a beret was painting at an easel. Another poodle rode a bicycle. There were also poodle ice skaters, roller skaters, joggers, and skiers. "Lots of poodles," said Nanda.

"Because they're so smart. Boxers are smart too. See the chef? And the string quartet? And how about that German shepherd directing traffic. Police dog, get it? Now one of my rarest dogs is that little black next to the Heinz with the hydrant. That's a Pulie—a Hungarian sheep dog.''

Drew thought it was time for their planned scenario. "Miss Egan? Did Nanda tell you that we're getting married next month?"

A blank look from Irene.

"It should be the happiest day of our lives, but last night we had terrible news."

Caution or anticipation, Drew couldn't tell which, filmed Irene's face.

"We planned it to be a double wedding with my cousin and her fiancé. Last night we learned that he had drowned."

No reaction.

Nanda stepped to Drew's side. "He drowned in Maine," she said. "Just off the coast of North Haven."

Not a flicker. They might be a dull TV show she was watching because she had nothing better to do.

"We came to you because you know him," said Drew. "David Benoit."

Paydirt. Irene's head snapped back and she stiffened as if hit by a killer bolt of lightning. Her hands grabbed the polished arms of the chair. Her eyes rolled, her jaw worked frantically. Nothing coherent came out.

"Water?" cried Nanda. "Should I get you some water?"

Irene shook her head no and pressed a hand against her breast. When she could speak, her voice was whispery. "I just wrote to David. I just sent him a letter."

"I know," said Drew. "I read it. This accident is terrible news, but we were sure you'd want to know."

"He was such a good friend."

"In school, you mean?"

"Not just school. He was a pen pal."

"How could he be a pen pal if he never wrote back?"

"He was a real big shot. He didn't have the time. It was enough for me to know he was thinking about us here. And of course I wanted him to know we were thinking of him."

"We? You mean other people in Coker Falls?"

"Just me and my dad. Until he passed away."

"I understand your father was injured in that accident at the mill."

"Yes. I took care of him. Night and day—ask anyone."

"The accident was Frank Benoit's fault, wasn't it?"

"That's what they say."

"And David's fault too?"

"David's? Why?"

"Why not? The sins of the fathers are visited upon the children."

"Sins? But David was such a goody-goody."

Drew was getting tired of this. "You had to blame someone. Frank Benoit had run away, so you went after David."

"Me? Never. He was just a kid."

"A kid who got out. You had to stay. You had to quit school and take care of your father."

"I did a good job. No one could of done better. Ask anyone if you don't believe me."

Nanda cut in. "I believe you. I believe everything you've told us. Every word."

Drew got her message. No more. Dry well. Crazy person.

Again that curious blurring or filming of the woman's heavy features. Drew realized it was a smile. It was what she did when she smiled.

"Let me tell you, it was no bed of roses."

"Of course not," said Nanda quickly. "Look, we have to go. Thank you for an interesting afternoon."

"You're leaving?"

Nanda didn't so much answer as float herself and Drew out the door on a babble of white noise.

Halfway to the car, a bunch of neighborhood kids staring, they heard the peremptory call.

"Miss? Miss?"

Nanda turned.

"If you see any special doggies down there in Massachusetts, I hope you'll remember me."

"Don't worry," Nanda called back. "I will."

Moving fast, she was soon in the car. "Drive," she told Drew.

Take me, he thought she meant, back to Cathy and sanity.

But at the corner she asked him to turn right, not left. Her chin was high. "I want to comprehend this joint. The environment that produced Newell Coker, Frank Benoit, Irene Egan, and the child-beating Fourniers."

In rapid succession they passed a blocky brick school, a Congregational church whose graceful steeple needed paint, a meager, newer Catholic church, a gas station, some mobile homes that weren't moving anywhere, ever.

That seemed to be the end of Coker Falls until a bend in the road revealed Mario's. Schlitz signs glowed red in each of the three low windows. For the first time, Nanda spoke. "I was wondering about nightlife."

"So was I." Drew made a wide turn into the parking lot.

They'd been climbing, and Coker Falls lay spread out below. "Look at the falls," he said. "They've installed a new turbine. Speaks well for the current management."

Slow-motion, she turned to face him. "I'm not ready for turbines. I can't handle transitions that fast. Why women aren't corporate presidents, I guess."

"Nobody here is a corporate president," he said. "Let's stretch our legs."

Instead of answering, she jumped out and walked rapidly to the lip of the parking lot.

Mario's afternoon customers were represented by a battered Subaru, two pickups and a late model Trans Am. The air, this far from the mill was almost fresh.

Nanda turned to Drew and produced a woebegone smile. "I want my life real, without illusions. But reality keeps doing me in."

He put his arms around her and spoke into her hair. "It does me in too. I needed to see something good in this horrible place, so I saw the turbine."

Neither one had the sense of supporting the other—or of being the first to break away. They simply regained their own two feet, a little dazed, not much to say. Yawning, smiling, dying for a beer, they made for Mario's.

Several drafts and a pizza with everything later, they'd learned more about Coker's Falls. The present owner was a grandson of Newell Coker's named Warren Whiteside. Business was good, damn good. Turns out this so-called paperless electronic society uses more paper than ever before in the history of mankind.

Frank Benoit? Frank was the last of the old-time bosses. Don't make 'em like Frank anymore. David? Wasn't there two boys? The youngest? All right, then, he was the one that joined the Navy right after the accident. Serious kid. Altar boy. His mother wanted him to be a priest.

Irene Egan? Oh sure, everyone knows Irene. After her old man died, Whiteside let her work in Accounting until she screwed up the whole department. Now she's in Maintenance. She comes in to clean when she feels like it, don't when she don't. A character, Irene. Talk your ear off. You should see her dog collection. Hundreds of china dogs. Kinds you never heard of. A real dog? You kidding? Real dogs chew the furniture, make a mess. Irene likes things clean. Kept her old man clean as a baby.

Drew stopped at a highway phone to call Pen. He was on a deadline, people yelling in the background, but he had to hear every detail. Some twice. At that, Drew wasn't sure his cousin had accepted what no longer seemed debatable—Coker Falls was innocent.

Chapter 17

Nanda walked to work Monday morning feeling as if she wore a sandwich board: WARNING! THIS EMPLOYEE CONCEALS VALUABLE INFORMATION. David Benoit was probably dead. He and Pen Mauran had probably been lovers, not that this had any bearing on his disappearance or anything else, unless of course it did. . . .

It filled her head like static. Would anyone at Hammond, Halsey ever believe she hadn't blabbed company business to Drew?

The worst had been lunch Sunday. They were at a Mexican place in Portland. The question they'd been avoiding since he'd picked her up at Cathy's was on the table. Did David drown or did someone drown him?

"Cathy says there's dope traffic on the coast. Maybe he saw something he shouldn't have."

"Maybe."

"It's really deserted where they found the boat, she says. Little islands and mucho places to hide. Good for dope transfer."

"I'd be happier if I knew why David left in the first place. There he was, chief architect of the IPO, working full speed, thriving on it. Then suddenly he's off, incommunicado. Makes no sense."

Nat Partridge had told Nanda it was overwork and stress. But was she supposed to mention this outside the firm? "At least we know one thing," she said instead. "Coker Falls was a big fat problem for him. Irene's last letter might've come at just the wrong time."

"I've been wondering if something happened at Dynagen on Monday or Tuesday morning. A fight of some sort."

Tuesday, Nanda thought. The meeting that kept Nat from helping her with Coleman Boone. "Will you be seeing Nat Partridge at your club tomorrow night?"

"Probably. Guy's a clock."

She frowned but said nothing.

His smile was gentle. "I don't talk to Partridge any more than the form requires. Never have. There's no reason he or anyone else will hear about this weekend."

"It's not just this weekend. God, what a mess."

He waited for more.

She sighed. "The easiest thing would be to stop seeing each other right now."

"I can come up with plenty of things easier than that. Easier for me, anyway."

She didn't want to play. "If we keep seeing each other, we'll be *seen* seeing each other. And if it comes out that Pen's your cousin, I have to be able to tell everyone at work that I've never talked company business with you. Never *ever*—outside of Paladin, of course."

"Fine. Makes perfect sense."

"It cuts both ways. I can't tell them what I know about David any more than I can spy on Dynagen, even to help you."

"Absolutely."

"Oh."

"Okay?"

"I'm not sure."

"Better, though."

It was. Which was why she felt the way she did about him. He kept making things better for her.

At her door, she said she wouldn't ask him in. "God no," he'd said, pretending to be horrified. "We've been in each other's pockets all weekend. We need our space."

"Not that," she said. "Tomorrow's on my mind. You'll be sending over the term sheet on Paladin. What if I have to question something? Drive a hard bargain?"

"So you want a quiet evening. A good night's sleep."

"Exactly."

"Do you realize you're giving me the identical advantage?"

If he couldn't be with her, he'd just said, he'd be alone. And even if this wasn't entirely true—he'd surely have to spend some time with his cousin—he'd been generous to put it like that. Getting-to-know-you stuff had its weird side. You had to be careful. You couldn't bang right out with things, no matter how much you needed to know about other women.

But he'd more or less said there weren't any other women. And once again made things better for her. If it wasn't so soon and all, she'd think she was falling in love.

"Morning, Nanda."

Her heart banged, but Wink Halsey passed by without further comment. Wink loved Mondays. Another weekend of domestic lockstep had been survived. Four full days of freedom stretched ahead before the next round of cocktail parties, brunches, lunches, mixed doubles, dinners, and nightcaps.

"Do I hear Nanda?" Charlie Hammond called from his office. "Stop in a minute, will you?"

Her sandwich board sprouted neon lettering. All Charlie wanted, though, was for her to come along tomorrow when he visited Graphlog.

Leaving him, she walked right into Nat Partridge.

"Morning, Nat."

"Morning."

Well? she asked herself once she was safe in her own office. Well?

She'd gotten away with it.

When he was eating his HoJo breakfast in Augusta, Drew had found a one-paragraph story on a back page of the local Sunday paper.

Police say there is still no trace of David Benoit, whose untended sloop was found in Black Ledge by lobsterman Luther Raines last Friday. Benoit is a resident of Brookline, Mass.

According to Pen, there'd be nothing more unless the body was found or one of the wire services made the Dynagen connection. Pen himself was still too mad at the *Globe* to tell the news desk what he knew.

But Monday morning, by bizarre coincidence, the business section of the *New York Times* had a big story on Dynagen.

Sam Pardee had brought it in and spread it on Drew's desk. There was a picture of Cantrell and Morse wearing their lab coats.

"Photogenic," said Drew, indicating Cantrell.

"It's mostly about Medimex and Victor Chu. But listen to this. 'David Benoit, Dynagen's Chief Financial Officer, praises Chu's marketing acumen and says he complements the research strength of the rest of the Board.' Sad, huh? Present tense for a man who's been washed overboard? I guess the news isn't out."

"Guess not," Drew said, leaving it at that.

Last night he'd found Pen at home with some friends. He hadn't stayed long and no one tried to keep him. He told himself that Pen needed to be around men who understood what he was going through in ways he, Drew, could not. Which was, he later decided, a highly arguable premise. He'd like to argue it out, but not this morning and not with Sam.

"I just thought of something. Does Hammond, Halsey know the boat's been found?"

"They didn't hear it from me."

"No special reason to tell them."

"No." Drew scanned the article. "Here's Fraker. 'My preference is to till ground already broken, but I couldn't resist this one.' "

"Makes him sound like some kindly old dirt farmer. When's someone going to call this guy for what he is?"

"Think Paladin'll catch his fancy?"

Sam threw up his hands.

Drew's phone buzzed. "Mrs. Spellman," his secretary said.

Sally had never called him at work before. Drew flashed on his old girlfriend Caren. On all his old girlfriends. "Sam? It's personal."

Sam's rapid scuttle for the door told Drew that his Spalding episode had been only forgiven, not forgotten.

"Hi, Sally."

"Guess what?"

"You won Megabucks?"

"Next best. I'm a rich divorcée. He signed."

"Sally! That's wonderful."

"You're the fourth person to know. First was my sister, second was my travel agent, third was Atlas Van Lines. I'm leaving Thursday. My sister's got it all lined up—location, chef, the works. We're practically in business."

She told him some more about the restaurant, and he told her some more about how good it sounded. Then there was a pause.

"Feel like celebrating?" he asked.

"Sure. Our best way?"

"Absolutely."

"Tomorrow night? I'll be exhausted from packing, but what the hell."

They settled it and hung up. Much as Nanda was the woman he longed to be in bed with, Sally had been a good, true friend. If she wanted this kind of send-off, he'd be churlish to turn her down.

Bird in the hand? That too, he admitted.

Just after noon a messenger handed Nanda an envelope bearing the Blackstone logo. Drew's cover letter was addressed, correctly, to Nat and her together.

She looked for a separate personal note before she realized there wouldn't be one.

The term sheet, four pages long, dealt, as usual, with the holdings of stock, its conversion from preferred to public shares, the structure of the Board of Directors, and other matters of the new company's financing.

Having reviewed a number of typical Hammond, Halsey term sheets just that morning, Nanda was immediately struck by a difference. Blackstone's sheet assumed Paladin's success. The others awarded equal time to failure and the cushioning of investor bailout.

She knew which version she'd go for, if she were Coleman Boone. But how would Nat react?

She buzzed him. He could see her at four.

*   *   *

At Nanda's entrance, Partridge slid a blank sheet of paper over the yellow pad he'd been writing on. He frowned at Drew's cover letter. "How was it this came to you?"

She kept her face pleasant. "My name was on the envelope."

"Wasn't mine?"

"Sure, but mine first, so the messenger gave it to me."

"Strange. Why would Blackstone do that?"

"Ladies first?"

"Well, no matter. I couldn't get to it then and I can't now. Tomorrow at the earliest."

"I'll be in all morning."

"Off in the PM?"

Nat had to know everyone's business. "Charlie asked me to come along to Graphlog."

Partridge produced a puckery smile.

"So if you and I," she went on, "could get together around ten? Or earlier?"

He consulted his pocket calendar, holding it up like a poker hand. "Nine sharp. I've got an important lunch."

Which meant he had nothing to do all morning besides wait for lunch. She also knew what the puckery smile meant. He was pissed that Charlie was trotting her out in public. Advertising the firm's reliance on one so young and female.

When men act like that, you simply kill them with confidence. Drives them totally bananas. "Nine it is," she said breezily.

Chapter 18

The locker room was a madhouse. The warm weekend had brought beach days closer, inspired yearnings for flat stomachs. Drew and Pen had finished swimming. Swaddled in towels, they drank a beer and waited out the rush on the showers.

Pen had called right after Sally, partly to invite himself for a swim but mostly to say that he'd sorted things through. "By the time David and I got together, he was ready to ditch the Irenes of the world, the whole self-hating guilt trip life had saddled him with. Try the sunny side of the street for a change. Then, before he can make it a habit, someone wipes him out. I'm going to find out who and why. No more tantrums and feeling sorry for myself. No more hallucinations about crazies in Maine and do-nothing cops. I talked to some regional guys at the paper. Maine has the lowest violent-crime rate in the entire U.S. It's also dirt poor. They budget their police departments for a symbolic deterrent and keep their fingers crossed. A thin manpower situation, they call it. So I'm joining the force. Poke around, see what's what. Maybe you'll come along. I'd like that. We'd be good together."

The showers at the Charles River Club were famous. Their old-fashioned perforated chrome heads, big as salad plates, released a thrumming stream just short of painful. When several were running at once, the din was formidable. Even so, splashing and soaping within it, Drew and Pen could hear the commotion that signalled Nat Partridge's arrival.

The backgammon players, whetted anew by the article in the morning's *Times*, were clamoring for inside poop on the IPO.

Drew turned off the water and grabbed a fresh towel. When

Pen did the same, they could hear Charlie Tucker's big-chested voice loud above the others. "Have a heart, Nat. Give us a ballpark, at least."

"Any reason why he should enjoy himself when David's under all that cold ocean?" asked Pen.

"None whatsoever."

They cornered Partridge in the middle of the short hall that connected the locker and shower rooms. His spoiled-boy face was flushed and happy.

"Rotten shame," Drew said, "about David Benoit."

Partridge blinked and reared back. "What's that you say?"

Drew said it again.

"David? What's happened to him?"

"Last Friday a lobsterman found his boat. The police think he drowned."

Partridge seemed to sag into himself, face in his hands. He pressed so hard his knuckles whitened. Then, with a strange sidling movement, he spread his fingers and peered through them. "Is this some kind of joke?"

Pen controlled himself. "Jesus Christ, man. We knew him personally. He was our friend."

"Oh. Yes. I'm sorry. But you see, we haven't heard a thing at the company. Not a word. We were concerned, of course. He'd promised to be back on the job today—the poor fellow really had been flat out, terribly overworked. No one grudged him his holiday, even if it looked like he was taking an extra day. But I don't say we weren't concerned. How, uh, how did you find out about his boat?"

"I was in Maine this weekend," Drew said. "Saw it in the local paper."

Partridge gave his head a long, slow shaking. "Awful news. I appreciate your telling me, Drew. And, uh—"

"Pen Mauran."

"Of course. We've seen you here before, haven't we? I'm afraid my wits are scattered. I really can't believe this. He was a young man!"

"We'll let you go," said Drew. "You'll be wanting to get to a phone."

"Yes. Yes of course. Thanks again."

Long-winded Jock Munroe had the locker room extension tied up. Partridge, soaked with sweat from his rowing, would have to use the phone in the chilly upstairs lounge.

"Man's going to catch his death up there," Drew said.

"I think we did that quite well. I feel better. Action, right? Plus, we found out the official line—David left because of overwork."

"We also found out Partridge thinks we're capable of sick jokes."

"How was his reaction compared with Irene's?"

"Hers was more spectacular."

"Okay. Let's talk more at dinner."

They were at Drew's, eating one of Mrs. Brown's brown dishes. Pen, tasting lamb, had decided it was shepherd's pie.

Their initial talk was about Dynagen's next move. Assuming David was dead, what about the IPO?

"They'll have to find a new finance man," Drew said. "And do some paperwork for the Securities and Exchange Commission. Good CFO's are hard to find, but the rest is no big deal."

"So the IPO's safe."

"Far as I know."

"Which means someone at Dynagen could be having his cake and eating it too."

"Huh?"

"Those guys who were at my house last night? They all knew David pretty well, and no one's thinking accident. Murder's the only explanation for the safety harness that makes sense to them. You know Bob Rosenthal? Sort of short, good laugher? He's a criminal lawyer. He was the first one to wonder if Dynagen had a reason for not wanting David back at work."

"Jesus."

"You never thought of that?"

"No. Not remotely."

"Be a businessman. What're some reasons you'd like to get rid of a star employee?"

Drew had to think a minute. "Dynagen switches tactics.

They're going for X instead of Y. David won't hear of it. Gives them until Monday to see the light.''

"What's his leverage?"

"He could call a press conference. Tell the world how bad they are for planning X. There's an environmental hazard, maybe. Chance of mutant genes escaping unless they stick to Y. Or—actually, this is more likely—it could be the degree of capitalization. The size of the offering. Maybe Morse and Cantrell are being too greedy.''

"Stuff like that wasn't ironed out long ago?"

"The founders might have given him bad numbers to start with.''

"The good doctors. You don't like them, do you?"

"I didn't like them at the time. I might have been wrong. A fifty-to-one return on investment encourages second thoughts.''

"The whole success of the IPO hangs on the miracle cure, right? What if it's a fake?"

"I doubt very much they'd be this far along with a fake. Their schedule could be too optimistic, though. Don't forget, everyone thinks Dynagen has a product that's halfway to the drugstore. Take away the imminent product and what's left isn't much. Yawns and analysts yammering about closing windows in biotech.''

"Windows?"

"Opportunities to hype it up and rake it in.''

"Why did you say greed was the most likely reason?"

"More likely than mutant genes, I meant. The whistleblower's a finance man, not a scientist. But now that I've started thinking this way, there's no end to what might have gone wrong. Lab models, bench models, can work beautifully. Then you scale up and there's a bunch of nasty surprises. Increased volume, increased speed of production—there's no end of troublesome variables. I think I mentioned my new company, Paladin? It looks like a winner, but we're a long way from full production.''

"Say you're prepared to be a whistleblower. You lay out your ultimatum. Don't you stick around to bug people? Every hour on the hour?"

"I would," said Drew. Anyone would. Look how Sally hung in, pestering her husband.

"So why didn't David stick around? Aside from that, though, the theory works. If David's dead, they can take X for an end run and no one will ever hear a word about Y."

"It works if you can imagine the likes of Morse and Cantrell committing murder." Or, Drew suddenly remembered, Harriman Fraker.

"They hired a gun. Happens all the time. Read the *Globe*."

Before Pen left, the cousins had settled on a plan of attack. Both had network possibilities in Maine—Drew among the Penobscot Bay summer colony, Pen through the *Globe* and what he called the great gay East Coast underground. They'd start putting out feelers right away. No point waiting around until David's body was found. Action was the way to go.

Drew was almost asleep when something snapped him wide awake. Pen, tonight, had seemed in good shape—steadier than he'd been since David first took off. It had been easy to sign on with him as teammate, networker, whatever else he had in mind. Besides, Drew felt he owed it to David.

But say the criminal lawyer was right and Dynagen wanted David gone. Say that and you're talking a level of debt that can't ever be paid.

Way back when, Drew had been within a hair of advising David to stick with Cavendish until he could find better men than Cantrell and Morse to hitch his star to. If he'd spoken up that first night in Pen's kitchen, David might still be alive.

Chapter 19

The following morning, a minute before nine, Nanda picked up her Paladin folder and headed for Partridge's office.

Mary Quinn, his secretary, was giggling into the phone. She let Nanda wait three beats too long before interrupting her friend's story. "He won't be back," she then said, "until after lunch."

"Are you sure? We had a meeting set for nine."

"All I know is he's at Dynagen until after lunch."

"I see. Take a message for him, will you?"

Nanda made the message a good long one, the telephone friend left dangling. Not much of a revenge, but better than bopping the bitch, sending her sprawling. Got more like Nat every day, Quinn did.

Taking his chair at the conference table, Partridge called it a good job well done. He'd hardly been off the horn since Lispenard dropped his bombshell, but the results were worth it. No question, getting these busy men together on overnight notice was a coup, a real coup.

Harriman Fraker had been literally plucked from the air—enroute to Phoenix, he'd ordered his pilot to make a U-turn back to Boston. Christopher Peale, the ambitious young investment banker from Norris, Pitney, had caught yesterday's last flight from Dallas, canceling, in the process, the breakfast meeting he'd flown down for.

The doctors, too, had responded to Partridge's bidding. Wade Cantrell, fiercely devoted to his son's school career, was missing the boy's performance in the class play. And Larry

Morse, for the first time in history, had shown up on the dot instead of waiting to be dragged bodily from his lab.

Missing were Victor Chu and Louis Ralli. Chu was spending the week at Medimex's manufacturing facility in Seoul. Dr. Ralli, Dynagen's guru, had not been invited. Last night, discussing strategy for the meeting, Cantrell had pointed out to Partridge that the matter before them was administrative, not scientific.

Neither Partridge nor Cantrell expected Fraker to cause trouble. Chris Peale, though, was a horse of a different color. Ambitious young investment bankers are thick on the ground. David had picked Peale to usher in the IPO partly because he, too, was a small-boat sailor. Partridge knew how suddenly these minor personal links can snarl things up. Peale, he'd told Cantrell over the phone, would require careful handling.

"Hold up there," Cantrell had responded. "Peale works for us, doesn't he?"

"Technically, yes."

"Well then, if misplaced loyalty to David obliges him to veto the new program, we simply fire his ass."

Appalled, Partridge hastened to explain that changing investment bankers would cause repercussions beyond belief. More trouble than David's disappearance, even.

"I'm not worried. Doesn't he have a fat bonus riding on this IPO? I think he'll see us through."

Partridge tried one more warning. Men had been known to rear up on their hind legs in righteous protest. He hoped Cantrell would bear that in mind.

Cantrell opened the meeting. "I know I speak for us all when I say that David Benoit will be sorely missed. His human qualities and his professional talents were exceptional. I think we're also agreed that our finest tribute to him will be the speedy and successful conclusion of the work to which he so tirelessly dedicated his last weeks."

Partridge nodded vigorously. Larry Morse, told by Cantrell to keep still unless questioned directly about MS-alpha or the vaccine development, said nothing.

"Hear, hear," Fraker growled. Eyes squinting, long, thin

mouth resolute in his fleshy face, he was lighting his first cigarette. No one else at the table smoked. Fraker's first act as an investor had been to torpedo Cantrell's proposal that their meetings be smoke-free.

Chris Peale leaned back in his chair and looked around the table in a way that reminded everyone but Morse that he'd played football for Yale. "Before we go any further, I'd like someone to tell me why I wasn't informed immediately when David left town."

Cantrell, expecting the question, had an answer ready. "We assumed he'd called you himself."

"Well, he didn't. Which is one of the stranger elements in this whole strange story."

"He wasn't himself, Chris. Don't blame him—blame us. We let him push himself too hard." Cantrell produced the shrug that had charmed TV audiences across the nation. "It's the Dynagen way, I'm afraid."

"I saw him Friday and he was fine—as fine as a man can be who's been putting in overtime. I told him he looked a little gray around the gills. He laughed and said it went with the territory."

Partridge spoke for the first time. "David always gave his best. It was a matter of principle with him. But Wade's absolutely right—we let him push himself too hard. I personally think he was overwhelmed by the prospect of the road show. It would be his first, of course—and for all his professional skill, David was essentially a shy and private man."

Peale, the veteran of a half-dozen road shows—those four- or five-day marathons that introduce new stock issues to key investment centers around the country—said no more. Even with a hot stock like Dynagen, the pressure was intense. You were up and selling every waking hour. You answered dumb questions as if they were smart and handled smart ones like porcupines. You ran constantly for planes. Meals were either missed or eaten in the inquisitive, not to say hectoring, company of potential customers. You had to remember everyone's name and be nice to bores. And manage, somehow, to move your bowels on schedule despite the total absence of privacy and peace.

Fraker ground his cigarette into the ashtray. "Do we know for sure he's dead?"

"With water that cold," said Cantrell, "you get a hypothermic situation developing pretty fast."

"But he hasn't been found."

"Not yet, no. I'm in touch with the authorities, of course. They'll call the minute there's anything to report."

Peale had never seen a drowned person. He had a sudden vision of David's body bloated, the hair streaming like eel grass. He cleared his throat. "The way I see it, we've got a number of related problems here. David is listed in the red herring as CFO. If he no longer holds that position, regardless of reason, this constitutes a substantive change. Wade, Larry, that means the prospectus has to be corrected. It's not insurmountable—we explain to Washington and they allow the alteration, hopefully without much delay. But then who's listed in place of David? We can't just bang in with a new CFO."

"Why not?" asked Fraker.

Peale kept himself patient. "Because, Harriman, David Benoit had a number of friends. Since his body hasn't been found, some of those friends might think we acted hastily."

"Balls. Like Wade said, we're only doing exactly what he'd have wanted."

Peale subsided with considerable internal effort but no more argument. He was an investment banker. Crass clients went with the territory, to quote poor David. He wasn't paid to reform them.

"Let me put a different spin on this, Chris," Cantrell said. "Good CFO's don't grow on trees. Finding David was a matter of many months."

Morse, believing that Cantrell was sanctioning delay, slid further down in his chair.

"What did Benoit have for staff?" Fraker asked.

"An accountant," said Cantrell. "Virginia Carmichael."

"Virginia?" It was as if Fraker had forgotten working women existed.

"Can she handle the road show?" Peale was worried. The smooth functioning of this event was on his shoulders as much as on Cantrell's—though God knows Cantrell, the glib sonofabitch, was worth his weight in whatever you measured. In MS-alpha, even.

"She's very young," said Cantrell, not adding that she was also very pregnant. "Our idea was to have Nat fill in on the road. He knows the financial picture as well as anyone—after David, of course."

Morse snapped into a normal sitting position. This plan was news, and he didn't like it. Once, early on, he'd heard Partridge blabbing away about MS-alpha like he'd invented it himself. Morse blew, right in front of everyone—Ralli, the other financial stiffs, everyone. Afterward, Cantrell had made a big noise, insisting Morse apologize. Morse said he'd quit first. Things got tense, but Partridge learned his lesson. His job was to provide money, not blabber. Now here was Cantrell offering to pay the man's airfare and hotel bills so he could blabber coast to coast.

The minute this farce of a meeting was over, Morse would have to straighten Cantrell out. Permanently.

Fraker shook out a cigarette and lit up, taking his time, keeping a hard eye on Partridge. "Unusual," he finally grumbled, "sending the venture capital guy around."

A lesser man, Partridge told himself, a man whose body was less perfectly honed and disciplined, would squirm and protest. I will merely regard the black dirt under Harriman Fraker's fingernails. I will think of that beautiful wife he bought himself and imagine those grimy hands caressing her face, combing through her smooth blond hair.

"Unusual," he replied, "but not excessively so." He leaned back, unconsciously imitating Peale. His voice had sounded fine. Leadership, as he'd always suspected, was a simple matter of packaging. Act like a leader and others will be forced to follow.

Peale had been reviewing his position. It was clear that those bozos intended to push the offering through on schedule. Further efforts on his part to delay at least until David's body was found would only give them fresh opportunities to screw up. They might, for instance, decide that Morse could be a road-show asset—that investors would be impressed by the spectacle of a brilliant scientist reaming out his nose and chewing on the findings. So. It was time for progressive thinking. What silk purses could he make out of those sow's ears?

"Let's agree there's not an ideal situation here," he said.

"We're looking for top dollar. For levels of investor confidence no one's seen in months. Essentially, we've got a closing window propped open by product one and product two in the pipeline. Now relax, Wade and Larry, we know MS-alpha is a dynamite product. But we better agree the window's got a powerful tendency to close. Okay. What've we got to fight that tendency with?"

He looked around the table, pausing on each attentive face. Even Morse was right with him. Good-bye, David. No one can afford to mourn you. "Momentum. The public's in our hand, thanks to Wade's good work with the media. They're champing at the bit."

Peale spread out his hands, palms up, nothing to hide except the gigantic home mortgage he'd signed last week on the strength of this deal. "So forget what I said about acting too hastily. We've got our momentum. Let's go for it. Let's pull Miss Virginia in as Acting Financial Officer and go for it."

Morse was on his feet, his mind racing down the corridor to the locked lab where his mice waited for his needles and measurements. The other men simply sat. Getting exactly what they'd hoped for had left them stranded.

"Virginia," Fraker sighed. "Christ. I thought women were just another fad."

"Poor David," said Cantrell. "I hope they find him soon."

"Maybe we should offer a reward," said Partridge. "Incentivize the lobstermen and whatnot."

Fraker snorted. "Couple of years ago my uncle capsized right off the family compound on Deer Isle. Squall. We searched for the rest of August. Never found a trace. The currents there'll sweep you straight to Portugal."

"Gotta go," announced Morse, halfway to the door.

No one was ready to follow. Heavy thoughts of death and profit nailed them to their chairs. Thoughts of Maine, too. Partridge had no use for the place, much preferring his grandfather's spread on the Cape. But like every other Boston boy of his upbringing, he carried around a mental map of Maine's major watering holes. Fraker's story stirred him profoundly. Deer Isle lay just east of the North Haven ledges David's empty boat had fetched up on.

Chapter 20

"The nerve," Charlie Hammond fumed, "calling this cow track a turnpike." He and Nanda, their meeting with Graphlog concluded, were crawling through the afternoon rush hour toward Route 128. "With the taxes high tech pays, you'd think they could build us a decent road."

Nanda murmured in sympathetic agreement. High tech had definitely put this formerly rural area on the map. Companies clustered in industrial parks—low-lying structures connected by common driveways. There were lawns, foundation plantings, basketball hoops. The pungent tang of wood-chip mulch saturated the air. But "industrial park," it struck Nanda now, was really a pun. Its essential meaning derived not from rhododendrons and wood chips but from acres of asphalt laid down for the parking of employee cars.

A bicyclist, lean, bearded, and helmeted, tiny reflecting mirror on the traffic side of his hornrims, passed them and was soon far ahead. "Boy has the right idea," said Hammond. "Assuming he survives."

Nanda had done well at Graphlog—well enough to reveal to her boss a little personality. "It's funny. Most of the people in this traffic jam work way out on the far edge of technology. The entrepreneurs spend their days inventing solutions to problems most people haven't even identified. Then, like sheep, they tolerate this insane traffic. Where's their entrepreneurial spirit before and after hours?"

"Huh. Never thought of it quite that way."

Too much personality. She backtracked. "Maybe they like it. At least they're safe from phone calls."

Hammond smiled. "No, you're onto something. Don't drop it too fast. We do tend to think of entrepreneurs as frontiersmen. Certainly that's the media image. But the longer I'm in this business, the more I think what really drives them is a need to prove something. They want to show the world. The best place to do that is on the edge, where no one's been before.''

"Once they're out there, they stop noticing what's in here?''

Hammond liked this. "Speaking of showing the world, your boy Boone's a textbook case. Everything okay there?''

"Blackstone sent the term sheet yesterday. Looks pretty straightforward, except that there aren't any covenants on the loan.''

"Then what's it secured by?''

"I guess by Blackstone's belief that Boone wants Paladin to succeed more than anyone else, including his financial backers.''

Hammond frowned. "What's Nat think?''

Don't whine, Nanda instructed herself. Don't tattle. "Soon as he gets loose from Dynagen, I'll let you know.''

"Might be a while. They've got their hands full out there.'' Hammond sighed. "You better hear the whole story. David Benoit—you know, the CFO—suddenly decamped for a week of sailing. Apparently he was so stressed by the upcoming road show he needed a vacation. The coast of Maine isn't my idea of an early spring holiday, but to each his own. Anyway, the poor fellow seems to have gotten himself drowned. It's not on the news yet. Nat ran into a couple of Benoit's friends and heard it from them. Then, he spent last night setting up a strategy meeting. Apart from the personal tragedy, we're worried about the IPO. I sure hope Nat's doffed his thinking cap.''

"You know the Ninnys!''

Hammond had no idea what she was talking about.

"You just quoted Vinnie Ninny.''

"Good Lord, did I? My kids loved those books. I bought one for my grandson just yesterday.''

It was, for Nanda, a short respite. Hammond returned to Dynagen's difficulties for the rest of the ride. She listened carefully, full of guilty dread, but the only thing she didn't know already was that Drew must have told Nat about David. How, she wondered. And why? She'd love to know, but asking would break her own rule.

Back at the office they found Partridge waiting for them, all charm and contrition.

"I filled her in on Benoit, Nat."

"Good." Partridge smiled at Nanda. "The least I could have done was call you and cancel."

"No harm done." Nanda said. "Let's meet soon, though."

"Do you have a minute right now?"

She said she did and they went into his office.

Mister Cooperation, she thought. Putting on a show for Charlie.

She was wrong. Nat had studied the term sheet and was satisfied. "Not quite our way of doing business, of course. I considered trying to get us some concrete protection, but it's not worth it. We lose time and we might lose face. Blackstone's got the lead, they can make the rules. Wink and Charlie sometimes forget that. I'll make a point of reminding them."

Nanda, flabbergasted, thanked him for his help. "I'll call Blackstone right away—unless you'd like to."

"No, no, you go right ahead. I've got to catch Charlie up on Dynagen. Cross your fingers, but we might be out of the woods."

"That's great, Nat."

Her warmth seemed to startle him, and she left without further comment. The poor jerk, she decided, has held up one too many APPLAUSE cards for himself. He earns the real thing and he can't handle it.

But what a terrific afternoon! Aside from two million guilty pangs about Dynagen, everything had worked out. She'd saved Paladin from Nat—saved the whole deal, really. Nat's idea of concrete protection was to suspend an entrepreneur from his own Board of Directors until the payback delinquency was satisfied. Suppose he'd wanted this written into the term sheet? Nanda could imagine Coleman Boone's reaction. Not to mention Drew's.

And now she would call that darling man and tell him the news.

Her heart jumped. They were on their way. And much, much closer to bed.

Chapter 21

More than two weeks had passed since Luther Raines found the *Becky T*. There was still no sign of David's body—or that his disappearance was hurting the IPO.

Newspaper coverage had been confined to the logical sequence set forth in Dynagen's press release: stress, much-deserved holiday, accidental drowning. Maine TV gave it ninety seconds, Boston TV a minute, the national networks zero. If any of David's friends in finance or high tech were shocked by Dynagen's hasty appointment of Virginia Carmichael, they kept it to themselves.

A hiccup, then. Allowed its brief moment and smothered instantly by the real Dynagen story, the fun story of steak and sizzle, of miracle cure and the hottest IPO action ever witnessed on Planet Earth.

It was Sunday night, halfway into May. Pen had been to Maine and wanted to talk about it. He invited Drew to supper and told him to bring Nanda along. "One, I want to meet her. Two, she can do me a favor."

"She won't spill anything on Dynagen," Drew warned. "And she doesn't know David's gay."

"Or me either? Tell her before she gets here, okay? I hate to watch their little faces fall when they catch on."

They were in the kitchen, eating Chicken Carcassonne, a corn-and-green-pepper stew Pen had invented.

"Why Carcassonne?" Nanda asked.

"The base is leftover carcasses. My endearing Yankee thrift."

The cornbread was homemade too. Drew asked Pen if he ever baked muffins.

"Once in a blue. Why?"

"My muffin source moved to the Sunbelt."

"I'll give you some recipes. Hold everything. I've got it. Geoff West. You're Geoff West's baby sister."

"Drew must have mentioned it."

"Not at all. The minute you walked in I knew I'd seen you before. Not many people's eyes match their teeth. It's been driving me crazy. You had long braids, right?"

"Are you sure Drew didn't tell you?"

"Scout's honor. How's old Geoff?"

"He's fine. You look familiar to me, too, but I think it's mostly because of Drew. If you grew a beard, you could be twins."

"If *I* grew a beard? Listen to her. My activist friends want Drew to shave so we can make a poster. 'Which of these boys is bent?' sort of thing."

Nanda's chin lifted. "Might raise some consciousness."

"Except I'm not an activist."

"I see."

"Want to hear about my trip to Maine?"

He didn't have much to report. He'd seen the *Becky T.*, back, now, in her winter cradle. The hole the ledge had stove in the hull was no bigger than his arm. Repair would be simple. Everything else was shipshape, the safety harness right where it should be. Spurling, the boat-yard guy, had dried and stowed the sails.

"Which weren't torn, *nota bene*. Spurling halfway admitted a real storm should have done more damage. I freaked him out, by the way. David's sleeping bag was in this net thing over his bunk. I saw that big orange billow and I had to wrap up in it awhile. Spurling heard me howling in there."

Nanda reached out to grip his arm. "Who cares what he heard?"

"Yeah." He heaved a deep breath. "After that—well, after that I did some drinking with a down-and-dirty buddy who runs a motel near the boat yard. We're everywhere, you know. *Everywhere.*"

He looked at Nanda, who looked right back. Drew hoped this would stop soon.

"The next day I traced David's movements, starting with his call Tuesday morning to Spurling. It's all here, times and places."

He unrolled a chart that he'd marked, weighting its edges with the salt shaker, the pepper grinder, and the bottle of lecithin pills he swore by for memory enhancement.

"Next I called on Luther Raines. Luther's a real solid citizen. I put it to him. The peace and safety of this coast is in the hands of men like yourself, I said. No dice. Tight as a clam, old Luther. My down-and-dirty thinks he's afraid to set me on a trail that'll end at some local kid who runs drugs. Which is what your friend in Augusta thinks, right? What's her name, again?"

"Cathy Pettit," Nanda told him. "David might've seen something, was her idea."

"Okay. Now Luther was by no means the only clam I tried to pry open. I went through six or eight people in Hackett's Cove before someone would say definitely that David had spent the night there. It looks like the drug industry has spooked the whole coast and what we need is a mole. A sneaky underhanded paid informer. Think Cathy might help us find someone around here"—he drew a circle on his chart—"who needs work? Good pay, no heavy lifting?"

"I'll ask," said Nanda.

Pen was on his feet immediately. "There's a phone in here."

While Nanda was out of the room, Drew filled his cousin in on recent gleanings from his own network. "Best of all," he concluded, "guess who's spent every summer of his over-long life on Deer Isle? None other than Harriman T., for Tapeworm, Fraker."

Wednesday morning, Cathy called Nanda back with the results of her search for a mole.

"Alton Amy. Like Amy Carter. He's fifty-two, separated. Lives right in the town of Vinalhaven, which is on Vinalhaven Island. His wife moved to the mainland a few years ago. She sends him money and he picks crabs, but he could use some extra. His hobbies are hanging out and listening in on fishermen's shortwave. If this blows up, you never got it from me.''

"It won't blow up. Mr. Amy wants work, we want to hire him. Why's he so marginally employed, by the way?"

"He used to fish."

Nanda heard evasion. "Something you don't want to tell me?"

"Well, people are prejudiced. He's in a wheelchair. Multiple sclerosis. His brain's fine, but—"

Nanda assured her she understood.

She called Drew, but he was in a meeting. On impulse, she tried Pen at the *Globe*.

"What a nice surprise."

"Cathy found us a mole. A prospect, anyway. Alton Amy."

"As in Amy Lowell?"

Never underestimate a Harvard man. She laughed and told him about Amy's MS.

"Weird," said Pen. "Weird little coincidence."

"Isn't it."

"But good, on the whole. They're used to him being a busybody. What's Drew think?"

"Drew's in a meeting. I'll tell him when I see him later."

Saying this, her insides swam. The Paladin closing was scheduled for this afternoon. What would she become, freed from the stern knight who had monitored her chastity up until now? Was she at the end of one phase of life and the beginning of something deeper, richer, finer? Something she'd dreamed about but never known?

Her bodice-ripper language made her blush. She was glad Pen couldn't see.

The closing was over. As of this moment, Paladin was no longer a hope and aspiration but a company, a business.

They shook hands all around: Boone's lawyer, Blackstone's lawyer, Hammond, Halsey's lawyer, Partridge, Nanda, Drew, and Boone. Drew said computer invasion would soon seem as quaint as cattle rustling. Partridge said he could see the cover of *Forbes Magazine*, the chess knight in silhouette and Boone in full western regalia. In a clear, true baritone, Boone's lawyer sang the theme from the old TV series, "Paladin, Paladin, where do you roam?" Everyone laughed and shook hands again.

"Dinner tonight?" Drew asked in an undertone.

Nanda's knees buckled. Her fork was slick as raw egg, her heart a commotion. "Dinner would be lovely."

They ate at Rebecca's, on Charles Street, right around the corner from Drew's Brimmer Street apartment. The check had been paid, the change returned, the tip left. It was late, time to go.

Stand up, Nanda considered, and start walking. Easy as rolling off a log. She poured herself the last of the wine.

Drew gave her hand a squeeze. "Drink up. I planned a small surprise."

He looked so merry and confident she decided to act as if she trusted him.

In order to "keep it simple"—her phrase, her theory—they hadn't yet been inside each other's apartments. She knew his door, though, and thought they were walking farther along Charles than necessary.

"The surprise isn't at your house?"

"Wait and see."

They turned down Pinckney and headed toward the river.

"Is it a gold barge heaped with silken cushions?"

"Not exactly."

His arm close around her, he half swung, half lifted her up the two front steps of the Charles River Club. Before she knew what was happening, he'd unlocked the massive front door and pulled it shut behind them.

Pure glee, electric. She hugged herself, whirled around, hugged him. How had he done this? Was anyone else here? Can anybody just—no, of course they can't. But how *had* he?

"Hear that?" He pointed upward.

Someone was running a vacuum cleaner.

"That's Billy, my ally and fast friend. He'll be working up there until I ring him on the house phone."

"What about the other members?"

"Long gone."

She spun around from him and soft-shoed across the foyer's polished marble floor, stopping to run her hand over the linen-fold panelling on the wall. "Posh."

"Upstairs is. Downstairs no. What to see the locker room?"

"Oh my God. The main switching system of the Old Boy network. I can't stand it."

"This way."

He set the scene for her. The naked old men around the backgammon table. Nat Partridge bounding down the iron staircase, beating his arms across his chest *huh huh huh*. The shower heads big as salad plates. "My locker," he said, opening it. "No lock, naturally. Only gentlemen here. Which makes the sudden appearance of this"—he dangled a women's Speedo, bright red—"rather rum, don't you think?"

Nanda thought she would die. "We can swim? We can actually swim in the Old Boy pool?"

He showed her where to change and got into his own suit.

"Good God," he said when she emerged. "Good *God* Nanda." He'd never seen her in anything more revealing than a dress.

But she was looking at him, her sassy grin fading into helplessness. "You," she said, her voice husky. "You."

They stood there, rooted, fifteen feet apart. If they touched each other, if they fell into each other's arms, the universe would melt.

Finally Nanda retrieved her grin. "Okay. Where's this pool you keep bragging about? And how about a pair of goggles?"

Drew's dive had a racer's efficiency. His strokes hardly rippled the water. His turn was flawlessly timed and smooth as silk. Showing off, he knew. He couldn't help himself.

As he finished his first turn, Nanda dived in. She chose his breathing side so she could watch underwater before he, turning, could watch her.

They passed each other in the middle of the pool. A fin, she thought. His cock—she'd seen it swell against the tight nylon of his suit back in the locker room—was like a ventral fin. Stabilizing in the water? In her, once she could trust him?

The thought wiped her out. She had to tread water, catch her breath. Losing time, she had hardly finished her turn before their paths crossed again. Now, with him on her breathing side, she could see him slow to watch her underwater approach. This let her catch up some, and their next crossing was closer to the middle of the pool.

Thinking it would be fun to match strokes, to swim in unison, Drew slowed again to watch the quick red go by.

He almost swallowed the pool. The red suit was gone. She was naked. A flash of belly and dark triangle and she was past him, swimming steadily away. Coughing pool, staying underwater with difficulty, he saw the most beautiful ass and legs in the world wink down the long green tunnel of the lane.

He shucked his own suit, tossing it somewhere, and made his turn. Now she was on his breathing side, free to look without being seen. Oh Nanda. Oh clever.

He swam fast, faster than he'd believed a man in his state could move. When he caught up to her he was on her breathing side. He fitted his stroke to hers and they came out of their turns together.

Their synchronized swim lasted only one lap. At the end of it they slid into each other, laughing, gasping, one hand clutching the rim of the pool or they'd drown for sure. Her nipples, beautifully pink, beautifully erect, snubbed into his chest. He thought he felt sparks striking. She wriggled slightly and his risen cock was clasped between her thighs.

Serious now, they floated lightly, deliciously sliding, tethered at lips and fork.

It was a long kiss. Not safe. They could drown and never know it.

"I love your surprise," she said.

"I love yours."

"Let's go now.

"My house? It's closer."

"Your house. Definitely."

Chapter 22

The following Monday Pen called Drew at home, early enough to interrupt his breakfast. "They found someone. Same watch and clothes."

"We'll go together."

"Has to be right now. And after, I'm flying over to Vinalhaven. Got to get Amy activated. I was going to call him, but face-to-face is better."

"I'll pick you up inside of twenty minutes."

Sam and Rob would squawk about the short notice, but it couldn't be helped. Family came before partnerships.

First he'd call Nanda, though. It had been an amazing weekend, spent mostly in bed. He liked everything about her—her smells and tastes, the tears that clumped her eyelashes after orgasm and rolled down her cheeks when she laughed hard. She had a prim side, an enclosed fastidiousness about herself that alternated with the sexy inventions that had nearly drowned him in the pool. He loved her sexiness, but no more than he loved the alternative. He hoped it wasn't shyness, something temporary. He wanted it to be a contrast that would last forever.

She'd left late Sunday afternoon. Wouldn't even let him walk her home. "Got to get my office face back on," she'd said. "Tone down the fleshpot aura."

"I missed you," he said into the telephone.

"Did you."

He felt slapped. Does putting on your office face make you talk in a cold, bitchy voice? But you don't ask a woman a question like that unless there's plenty of time to hear the answer. Instead, he told her that David had been found.

Her response, he thought, came a little late. She said all the right things, but the tone was off. He might be a remote acquaintance.

"Did I wake you?"

"God no. I just came in from the river."

"Bicycling?"

"Yes."

Pulling teeth. "I'll call you when I get home. We'll probably have to spend the night up there."

"Tell Pen I'm sorry, okay?"

"I will."

"Bye," she said, and hung up. On him? Not exactly. Close enough, though.

A call to Rob, covering the appointments and business he'd have to miss, ate up the rest of his minutes. He had to leave right now. No time to call Nanda back, demand to know what the hell kind of hair she'd gotten across her ass.

But his year with Sally, away from the games of pursuit, capture, and strategic withdrawal, had made him an honest man. It wasn't time that prevented him from calling her back. The truth of the matter was that he didn't care what was making her act like this. The only thing he wanted was for it to go away. For her to be his again, the way she was yesterday.

It doubled him over, he wanted this so badly. It would kill him to hear that cool voice saying the weekend had been great fun but there was more to life than mere weekends.

He couldn't risk it. The brash young risktaker couldn't take a chance of that magnitude.

Fog, at times heavy enough to slow traffic, covered them all the way up the coast. Unless it lifted, their flight to Vinalhaven would be grounded. There was a ferry, a long, slow compromise, but who knew if they could get on it?

Every thirty miles or so, Pen would start again—This fucking place, worst fucking climate in the world, no wonder they're all rednecks and losers, probably waiting with shotguns, no, chainsaws, Spurling's put out the word I'm a dangerous pervert.

The address Pen had been given took them to a large white

clapboarded house with a Victorian mansard. The short walkway from street to front door was lined with chairs, commodes, coat racks, and whatnots—substantial, machine-turned pieces in golden oak. The sun porch was crammed to the rafters with china and glass.

"I must have written it down wrong," Pen said.

"No, look." Drew pointed to a small sign directing them down a second walkway to the rear of the house. Makes perfect sense, he thought, the undertaker being in the collectibles business. Who has better access to sources?

At the rear stoop, Pen suddenly halted. "Despise me if you want. I'm taking your offer."

If David was too bad to look at, Drew would say so. That was his offer. The challenge to despise was one of Pen's verbal tics, not worthy of response.

Ring and enter, said a second small sign. The waiting room was crowded with more golden oak and paneled in plywood. Scenes o' Maine calendar art decorated the walls. After a moment, Vernon Cardwell, undertaker and antiquarian, entered from the main part of his house, stuffing his shirttail in over his belly. The room's stale air notched up with Cardwell's arrival. Some old-timers are best encountered outdoors.

Drew introduced himself as a friend of the deceased.

"Mr. Mauran's my cousin. He's waiting outside for the time being."

"Don't blame him. Crabs got the face pretty bad."

Their next stop was Spurling's boatyard. Driving there, Pen couldn't leave it alone. "I should have gone in to him."

"No."

"To see what happened to his head."

A nasty crack on the forehead, Cardwell had called it. "The medical examiner will see it. You don't have to."

"I should have said good-bye."

"It's better to remember him the way he was."

"How can I be sure of that?"

"How'd you be sure if you'd seen him?"

Pen groaned. "Pain. I trust pain."

"Is that what you had together? Pain?"

"It's what I have now."

"Then you don't need any more."

"It's too final, is all."

He was right about that. When the medical examiner finished his work, Vernon Cardwell would turn David's poor gnawed and bloated body to ashes. Pen and whoever else wanted to come would then scatter these remains on an outgoing tide. Pen knew exactly where to do it. Methodical, orderly David had marked the spot on the chart last summer. The way Pen described it, Drew knew that this was a special place. Something important—a decision to spend the rest of their lives together, maybe—had been settled there between them.

Spurling gave the cousins a startled glance—holy doodle, *two* of them?—and never met either man's eyes again.

"I'm not ready to talk repairs," Pen said. "We're just here for a quick look."

Visibly relieved that no more was wanted from him, Spurling told them to take their time.

Pen gave the splintered break in the hull a tender caress. "David would have hated this. Anything broken or messy. Why I had to stop bashing down walls."

They hoisted themselves up. Pen opened the companionway and pointed to the sailing harness that hung right inside. "Exhibit A, if the dumb fucks would listen."

The cabin was scrupulously clean and tidy. Drew thought they should look for something. Clues. Like what? An alien strand of hair? Lint from the pocket of a lab coat, the kind worn by genetic engineers?

Then something occurred to him. When Pen was ready to leave, he went to find Spurling.

"I was wondering about the sails. Where were they taken off?"

"Right at Black Ledge. Harbormaster would've seen to that. You're towing, you don't want canvas blowing around."

"Meaning?" asked Pen in the car.

Drew shrugged. "In order to drown accidentally while sailing, you need sails. Just running down a foolish hope."

Pen grunted. "Look at that blue sky. You still up for Vinalhaven?"

Drew said he was. "Plenty of time for the cops first. You still up for that?"

The police station was manned by Sergeant Paul Crowley, who sat at the desk behind a large glass window, presumably bulletproof. Given the sleepy small-town context, this was bizarre enough. The faulty intercom made it Twilight Zone. Every question had to be shouted.

Crowley radiated lean, mean toughness. Drew would bet anything that he'd volunteered for Vietnam, maybe twice. The police department of a town of five thousand would be tame by comparison, even if summer quadrupled the population with city idiots like the two standing before him now.

Crowley logged them in and pecked at his computer keyboard. He frowned at a monitor whose face they couldn't see. He pecked some more, read again. Then he said what the law had been saying all along. If the medical examiner found anything suspicious, there would be an investigation.

"There's a nasty crack on his forehead," Drew shouted, deliberately using Vernon Cardwell's language. "Would you call that suspicious?"

"I might and I might not. What I'd do, I'd wait for the medical examiner."

It's hard to sound confiding and ingenuous at the top of your voice, but Drew did his best. "We're about to leave for Boston, and we just wanted to know if you had any theories. You personally."

"First off, you and Mr. uh, Mauran have to understand there's no, repeat no, sign of criminal activity. What we have here is an unattended death. Now, the mark on the forehead of the deceased. A man falling overboard could've hit his head on the gunwale."

Pen spoke for the first time. "That explains everything for you?"

"Explains the jib pretty good."

"What about the jib?"

111

"Loose, says here. Pennant was untied. He'd want that fixed."

In a low voice so Crowley couldn't hear, Pen asked Drew what the fuck a pennant was.

The short piece of line that holds the jib to the bow, Drew told him. "Very important. You untie it, all you've got's a flapping piece of cloth."

Pen turned back to Crowley. "Untied? Not frayed or broken?"

"Says untied."

"Why wasn't I told about this before?"

"Thought you was."

For once the intercom worked perfectly. "Wa-as," they heard—pure Downeast, tourists eat it up.

"Well I wasn't. And I'll tell you something else, Sergeant. David Benoit never tied a bad knot in his life. Never. Your theory stinks."

Crowley repeated his medical examiner line. Mr. Mauran should go home. "Any new developments on your 'friend,' we'll be in touch."

Pen heard the quotation marks. "Wondering when we'd get to that," he muttered. Then he erupted. "Why the glass, huh? You folks're so pure up here, why the glass?"

Into it he flattened his face, making a horror mask. Crowley flung his arms up in self defense.

Chapter 23

Alton Amy's house was not much more than a cabin set on a minute patch of level ground overlooking Vinalhaven harbor. With more land, a developer's dream. Drew, in his sailing days, had seen any number of these cramped little houses, built in an age when no one but fishermen considered the water's edge a good place to live. Windows were sized for protection, not views, and the tides took care of the family sewage.

Amy cracked open his door and rapidly sized up his visitors. "You two brothers?"

"Cousins," said Drew. He and Pen had argued about who'd do the talking. By pigheadedly repeating that he and he alone was responsible for Cathy Pettit's anonymity, Drew had won without having to cite Pen's loss of control in the police station. "We've come to offer you a business proposition."

"House ain't for sale. Neither's the land."

"Our proposition doesn't concern your property."

"Huh." But he wheeled backwards, allowing them to enter his parlor. More framed calendar art on the walls, enormous maroon plush overstuffed sofa and chairs, scattered newspapers and magazines. Along one wall a counter sagged with ham radio equipment.

Alton Amy had a lizard's quick, oddly lidded eyes and dry brown skin that paled, mid-forehead, where he set his baseball cap every time he ventured outdoors. He wore navy houndstooth check slacks, a knit shirt patterned in lime green paisley, and, on his no-longer-useful feet, clean white socks and polished loafers. A dapper little gent, Drew thought.

The first thing Amy wanted to know was how they got his name.

"My girlfriend Sally knows someone who works with your wife."

"That so? What's this someone's name?"

"I don't think Sally said."

"Huh. Well, no matter. Been a long winter, glad to see new faces. Not that I miss the wife, mind. Not with my lady friends banging on my door all hours."

"Can't blame them, can you? Like you said, it's been a long winter."

The three men exchanged sly smiles.

"I willed my wife my entire estate, you know. One condition—she's got to remarry. Yes siree. I want to be sure at least one man on this earth will regret my passing."

A triangle of uproarious male laughter.

Drew thought Pen might be reaching saturation.

"You're a busy man, Mr. Amy. We'll get right to the point. We need some information. We hope you'll use your radio setup and your knowledge of the area to help us. Now. Have you ever heard of MS-alpha?"

"Oh sure. Been on TV, you know. And my lady friends keep bringing me magazine clippings."

"Explain it was a coincidence, Drew."

"Good idea. We didn't seek you out because of MS, Mr. Amy. But I must say, it seems like a guiding hand is in there somewhere. Because one of the men who's worked hard for the drug drowned right near here. He was a good friend of ours. David Benoit. Maybe you know the name."

"Well you better *bet* I do. Know who found his sloop, too. And who found *him*. Friend of yours, huh? That's too bad."

"And very bad for MS-alpha that he's gone."

"I put my name in to be a guinea pig, you know. Wrote in just like Phil Donahue said. I'll chew up any pills they got, miracle cures, whatever. My lady friends're itching to dance with me. All right. What kind of deal you boys have in mind?"

Drew handed over what he had—a copy of the chart showing David's movements, a list of the people Pen had interviewed, and a list of the chief players in the IPO. That done, he settled into a tutorial mode, leading Alton Amy through the tactics, ethics, and economics involved in being an undercover mole.

Back on the mainland, a six-pack of cold Molson's Golden on the car seat between them, the cousins drove until they found some scenery. A calendar sunset filled the windshield.

"I have a feeling I'd like Amy's wife," Pen said at length. "Him I hate."

"He's a perfect entrepreneurial type. Mouthy, opportunistic, won't take no for an answer, and nobody's fool. Exactly what the job needs. Let's send him Irene's letters."

"Kidding?"

"Everyone she writes about has to be a Mainer. Might be a name in there he'll recognize."

"Bit farfetched."

"Too farfetched?"

Pen thought it over. "Maybe not. Once you accept the basic idea that Dynagen wanted David dead."

Then, after a pause, "Funny he wouldn't take money."

Amy had said they could give him a motorized wheelchair if they wanted, not that he needed it now and maybe never would, what with MS-alpha. "Be prepared" was his motto, though. The best chairs made come from California—got a brochure right here. Oh, and you can throw in one of those new cordless phones if it makes you feel less beholding. But nothing unless I deliver. I'm like that. Too proud to take nothing for nothing.

"Wouldn't take money? Did you read that brochure? The chair he's after costs close to four bills."

Pen had to laugh. "Guy's a wonder. You're right. Exactly what the job needs."

"You wiped? I'm wiped."

"Totally. My down-and-dirty'll give us a free room, but I can't handle his puckish charm tonight."

"Rob Kellner mentioned a place in Camden," Drew said. "An inn. Decent food and new mattresses on the beds."

Aside from a baloney on white, no lettuce, sole option of the airport vending machine, Drew had eaten nothing since his interrupted breakfast. Now he was haunted by visions of a lobster dinner—a full-scale *el turisto* blowout. Rob had described stuffed baked potatoes, baskets of sweet hot breads, homemade apple pie.

Drew's mouth flooded. He could see ice cream pooling on the pie's crust, trickling down the edges. And a motherly sort of waitress who'd throw in a bosomy cuddle while she was tying his lobster bib.

Pen had spurned the airport baloney. Drew hoped he wouldn't spurn dinner. Up against death and void, a man should pack himself with whatever was available.

Death, void, nothingness. Hard to remember that his own body, capable no less than David's of foul bloat, no less a potential feast for crabs, had known only joy and delight for an entire weekend.

Nanda. Her voice this morning had made it all history. The sunset was over too. He turned on the engine and headed for Camden.

Chapter 24

The inn served hearty breakfasts. Drew dawdled over his waffles and sausage, hoping to inspire Pen to eat more enthusiastically than he had at dinner. It didn't work.

Neither man felt like talking or music, so the drive back to Boston was quiet. In sight of the city's towers, though, Pen made an announcement.

"Amy's wheelchair? By me, chickenfeed. I'm a rich man. A brand-new millionaire."

"That right?"

"May not be right, but it's true. David's mother gets what she's been getting—which, believe me, is generous. Especially considering how minimally she performed when he was a kid. But his Dynagen stock and everything else is mine. Wonderful, isn't it?"

He was crying. Thinking of his own boyhood's guilty sorrowing, Drew was near tears himself.

They were coming up on the exit for Somerville and Dynagen, where David's personal office stuff, packed into boxes, waited for their pickup. Drew decided that their original plan to swing by, grabbing a quick look around, needed revision.

"How about I drop you at home, do the pickup on my own?"

A good idea. Pen didn't even bother to raise a token protest.

Dynagen was a single block beyond the Cambridge city line. Smart, Drew thought as he pulled into the parking lot that surrounded the low, L-shaped building. Morse and Cantrell had stayed close to scientific and medical centers without exposing themselves to the nuisance of a meddlesome citizenry. Somerville, unlike hypersensitive Cambridge, could be counted on to appreciate Dynagen's impact on the tax base and to turn a deaf ear to mutant-gene horror stories.

Drew parked next to the rattletrap Volkswagen bug Pen had

told him Morse had driven since his student days. The slot closest to the front door held Cantrell's sleek Jag.

Would a man kill to keep a Jag?

Pen had called Virginia Carmichael, so she was expecting Drew. He found her, vastly pregnant, in one of the offices that occupied the short leg of the L. It must have been David's office. The walls were still decorated with framed blowups of *Sail Magazine* covers showing grown men scrambling around wet decks. Macho hardship. No one falling overboard, though. No one hitting his head on the gunwale.

"Are you a sailor too?" he asked.

"No. Those are still up there—this is embarrassing— because they belong to us, not David. We paid for them, I mean. The lawyer's idea, but no one argued. It's so incredibly chintzy I won't take them down until someone else gets embarrassed enough to tell me to. By rights they should go to Pen right now. How's he doing?"

"Not great."

Virginia clucked her tongue. Pen, who had kidded around with her on the phone a couple of times, thought she had a pretty good inkling about him and David. A decent kid, he'd described her. Supported her husband, who was trying to make it as a serious musician. And not remotely a suspect, no matter how nervous she seemed at this moment.

Packing David's desk, she now exclaimed, had been her first official responsibility as Acting Financial Officer. "Everything neat as a pin, just what you'd expect. Extra neat, really. He must have cleared out his doodlings right before he left."

"Doodlings?"

"He was always jotting stuff down on the backs of telephone slips, whatever. Didn't have to be his own telephone slips, either. The secretaries would lose something—a letter, a report, and there it would be, upside down on David's desk, covered with scribbles. But all that kind of thing was gone, so I guess he chucked them."

She took Drew to a locked closet and showed him three sealed boxes. "There's a diskette in there marked Daily Log," she said. "It was in his PC. I figured it was personal so I didn't read it." She frowned and looked worried. "No one here knows about the diskette. I'd appreciate your discretion."

Drew signed his lips zipped.

Back in her office, she phoned the janitor and told him to bring around a dolly for the boxes.

"You've been at Dynagen quite a while, haven't you?" Drew asked while they waited.

"Since the beginning."

"Must be exciting for you."

"I'd rather have David alive and sitting here than be sitting here myself, if that's what you mean."

"I meant the excitement of the historical moment. The scourge of multiple sclerosis wiped from the face of the earth."

"Oh. Sorry."

"You know what I'd love? To see the lab."

"There're two labs. Maybe you can see the vaccine lab. That's Dr. Cantrell's. It's the busiest. More mice and all. The other lab is Dr. Morses and Conrads. And MS-alpha, of course."

"Conrad. Rings a bell. Didn't some woman try to get him fired?"

Virginia giggled. "Kim Dranchak."

By now Pen had told Drew everything he could remember David saying about Dynagen. Apparently this Conrad would wait until Kim Dranchak's hands were occupied by mouse and needle. Then he'd creep up behind her to snap her bra. When she stopped wearing a bra, he switched to the elastic on her underpants. Or so her story had gone.

"Whatever happened to her?" Drew asked.

"She quit. No one believed her, you know."

"David did. Or at least he told Pen he did."

"David didn't have to hear her other stories. Every day some new tale. Guys hustling her on the bus. Cab drivers making moves. A guy in church once, in the Confession line. That did it for me."

"The other women get along all right with Conrad?"

"No one pays any attention to him, he's such an old crab. Anyway, he and Dr. Morse work alone now that MS-alpha's on-line."

Thunder out in the hallway. The janitor with the dolly.

"Let's get the boxes in your car," Virginia said. "Then I'll see if Dr. Cantrell can show you around."

* * *

Cantrell was at his desk, going through a thick fan of green-striped printouts. Drew brushed past Virginia and strode right in, his hand outstretched. "Hi Wade."

Cantrell couldn't place him.

"Drew Lispenard, Blackstone Associates. I thought I'd say hello. Touch the historical moment, so to speak. The end of multiple sclerosis. You must all be very proud."

"Mr. Lispenard came to pick up David's things," Virginia explained, sounding apologetic.

Cantrell's expression was complicated. Drew let him dangle a moment before telling him he was acting for his cousin, Pen Mauran.

"That's all right Virginia. I'll see Mr. Lispenard out myself." He turned back to Drew. "The police called us this morning with the positive identification. A terrible tragedy. Such a waste."

"I know. And to think he'll never see his IPO fly."

"It's not fair, is it. We let him push himself too hard, I'm afraid. Of course we had no idea his stress was compounded by special pressures."

"Special pressures?"

Cantrell waved a hand. "His lifestyle."

"Ah."

Drew wanted to ask how they'd found out, but he had more important things to do. "I was thinking, since I'm here anyway, it would be great to have a look around your lab. Or Larry's."

"Dr. Morse doesn't take kindly to interruptions."

"Yours then. I'd like to tell my grandchildren I saw history in the making." He smiled winningly. "Course, I probably *won't* tell my grandchildren how dumb I was on that second-round financing. Boy, did David love giving me a hard time on that one."

"You knew David well, then."

"Yes."

"He spoke of his work here often?"

"Sure. That's why my cousin and I have a hard time believing he was stressed by it."

Cantrell dropped his eyes and gave his head a little shake. The hand that had been riffling the printout became suddenly clumsy. Means nothing, Drew reminded himself. Death makes everyone weird. Gay's no tranquilizer either.

"How about it, Wade?"

"How about what?"

"The lab tour."

Drew saw relief. Unmistakable relief that occupational and lifestyle stress had been abandoned as their subject.

"It will have to be a quick one. Our lawyer is death on outsider traffic. He's worried about lawsuits—the Agent Orange syndrome, if you take my meaning."

"Is there any danger of contagion?"

"Only in the sense that litigiousness is endemic these days."

Drew kept him talking along these lines while they suited up in white protective gear and put on masks. Once inside the lab, Drew did what detectives in books did—counted workstations and personnel and fixed the layout in his mind. Ventilating fans hummed steadily, and everything seemed scrupulously clean. Even so, there was a strong smell of droppings—like a long-closed vacation cabin, only worse.

The mice were caged in banks around the perimeter of the large room. The ones closest to Drew looked listless. "These guys sick?" he asked the pretty young technician who was working with them.

Cantrell cut in. "Some are. I can't be too specific. The vaccine development is top secret. And I'm afraid we've been in here too long as it is."

"Lawyer's orders. I understand. Thanks for your time. I feel as if I've learned something."

"My pleasure."

They were out in the corridor again. "Road show coming up soon?"

"Two weeks from tomorrow."

"Should be fun. Unless Virginia has her baby halfway through."

Cantrell's smile was thin. "Nat Partridge will be taking David's part in the road show," he said. "And now I really must get back to my desk."

"You bet, Wade. Thanks again. As I said, I really learned a lot from you."

Chapter 25

Delivering the boxes, making sure Pen wanted to be alone when he opened them, and describing the visit to Dynagen took a while. By the time Drew put his car away, it was almost five. Late enough to show up at the office in Maine clothes but still early enough to try making a dent in some paperwork.

He waved to Rob, who was on the phone, and interrupted Sam to tell him that the body had been David's and yes, it had been a long couple of days.

Slumped at his desk, Drew stared at his overflowing in-tray. Nothing like a shitload of paper to test the will of the weary. There was a thick sheaf of phone slips. Sorting listlessly through them, he suddenly snapped to. Nanda had called at two and again at four. The box next to Please Call Back checked in both cases, with Hammond, Halsey's number given.

She answered herself. "Oh. Drew. Good. Can you hold on a second?"

He heard a door close, then an indrawn breath released in two small whimpers.

"I wanted to say sorry for being such a jerk. There's a why, but maybe you don't care."

"I care."

"First, was it David?"

"Yes."

"And what about Pen?"

"Pen's . . . Pen's wonderful. We just got back."

"You're wonderful too. Want to hear my jerk story now or over a drink?"

"Over a drink, if you can give me until seven."

He was wonderful. He'd rip through this stuff like a super-sonic laser.

She looked so beautiful he had to hug her with his whole body. She stayed separate, prim. He reminded himself that he had liked this side of her.

She started by asking more questions about Maine.

He put a hand over hers. "Remember when we left Cathy's? You said you had to talk about something besides death? That's how I feel right now."

The waiter set down their bourbons. Seventy if a day. Everyone here was old. The last unyuppified bar in downtown Boston, running out the lease. Only place in blocks where a man wearing Maine clothes could get a drink.

They touched glasses. "Down with jerks," said Nanda.

"I'm going to wait and see," said Drew. "There may be a silver lining here."

Setting her up.

Instantly radiant, Nanda quoted Mother Ninny. " 'Silver linings do not show themselves until the surrounding clouds are very, very dark.' Mother was one smart lady. Okay, the story of my jerkhood. My brother Geoff and I usually talk Sunday nights. I call him or he calls me. This time I called him, mostly to brag about you." And to find out about muffins. Anything Patsy, Geoff's wife, didn't know about cooking wasn't worth learning.

"Once I finished putting a name on the mysterious figure I'd been spending so much time with, Geoff got very quiet. Then very tactful. I said stop bullshitting me, and finally he did." She drank some bourbon. "You've had some interesting girl-friends over the years."

Drew and Nanda were fully contemporary. Long before Paladin was signed, they'd done their AIDS show-and-tell. Both had recently and unproblematically donated blood. Nanda had mentioned her year with Tom. Drew had allowed Nanda to assume that grown-up, sensible Sally was typical of his taste in women. All's fair in love and war.

"Interesting? The one who tried to shoot my neighbors was interesting to the press. Other adjectives come to mind.

Spoiled. Theatrical. Nutsy. After the Libre episode—Geoff know about that? Yeah. A real crowd-pleaser, that one—my partners laid down the law. But I'd beaten them to it. It was fairly weird, how that happened. Little Spalding—I guess you heard it was a basketball—suddenly seemed like a good idea. Not Lally's little Spalding, but someone else's. Really shook me up.''

Not knowing whether to laugh at Spalding or kiss him for the rest, Nanda stuck to her guns. "So then why Sally? Why not look for a potential wife and mother?''

"Good question.''

"Maybe you didn't pick Sally at all. Maybe she picked you.''

"Something to that. She certainly knew her own mind.''

"But you picked the others. On what basis?''

"The usual. Gorgeousness. Sex appeal. A certain malleability which later proved fraudulent.''

Nanda nodded. Just what she'd thought.

"Except—'' Drew broke off.

"Yes?''

"Isn't this turning into the story of my jerkhood?''

She leaned across the table and touched his cheek. "Uh-uh. Mine. I got so snarled up with your record that I forgot something important. It dawned on me this afternoon—much too late to stop me from giving you that nasty send-off. Geoff convinced me you were trouble. You're not. You just pick trouble.''

"Didn't I pick you?''

"Course not. The instant you walked into Boston Proper I picked you. You could have been married, anything. Didn't matter. Your fate was sealed. I always get my man. And I *always* pick good ones.''

"Tom?''

"Sure. I said good, not perfect.''

Did any of this, Drew wondered, hold water? "One thing. A venture capitalist who has lousy judgment in people will make a lot of lousy investments. Which means he'll go broke pretty fast.''

"Far as I'm concerned, Drew Lispenard's the best judge of

men in the business. We're talking about something entirely different. Hammond, Halsey's yet to get a proposal from a woman. How about you guys?''

Very few, none in their usual areas of expertise. A curiosity of the trade. ''We've wondered where the entrepreneurial women are. Too far back in the pipeline, maybe.'' He grinned at her. ''You're saying that the scarcity of entrepreneurial women is what's been saving me from financial disaster.''

''Seems so.''

He traced her palm with his finger. ''It's a serious flaw. But if you keep quiet, no one will ever know.''

''No?''

''Who'd guess? Every man in this bar is jealous of me. They think I'm an excellent judge of women.''

''You keep doing that to my hand, we're going to have to leave.''

''Your house?''

''Yours is closer.''

''You always say that.''

''So far it's always been true.''

Chapter 26

"A treasure hunt with no clues and no treasure," Pen described the process of unpacking David's boxes.

The bulk was connected with personal finance. Tax stuff, bank statements, canceled checks. Everything neatly filed and labeled. This was a man who supported his mother, paid his bills early and lived well within his means. Mr. Clean. There was one book, *Walden*, falling apart from having been consulted so often.

"He marched to a different drummer?" Drew asked.

"More like every prospect pleases and only man is vile," Pen said. "We should shut up, rid ourselves of electronic diversion, and get down with nature."

"It's a theory."

"A theory that sent him off to die in clean green Maine. I shouldn't blame Thoreau, though. Hit men work cities too."

Knowing David's habit of commandeering stray pieces of paper, Pen was positive the doctors had gone through and cleaned these out. "His scribbles are hard to decipher. They'd be taking a real chance, leaving anything around."

The doctors, Pen was equally convinced, had overlooked the diskette. He'd printed it out on the system David kept at home. It began with the new CFO's first day at Dynagen and covered every weekday since with only two gaps. One was their sailing vacation. The other was his final Monday and Tuesday on the job.

This second gap, the cousins decided, was highly significant. David's office log, no less than the one he kept aboard the *Becky T.*, represented a fixed daily ritual. Why would a man so strict about ritual suddenly let go?

"Something bad happened Monday."

"And Tuesday he handed in his ultimatum."

It seemed the only explanation. And because there was nothing strange about the previous week's entries, the bad news had to have come from the blue. A development of the weekend, most likely.

"And get this," said Pen. "In the entire year, there isn't a single crack at Cantrell and Morse."

"He criticize anybody? Harriman Fraker? Nat Partridge?"

"Nope. There's a lot about drafting the red herring. NP—Partridge, I assume—objects risk clause 3, and like that. But David's not irritated. He doesn't say NP's a total asshole."

Drew heard something. "David's word against mine?"

"Kidding? I've experienced Partridge too, you know."

Drew waited.

"He was moving in! We were a couple! Why *can't* he say NP's a total asshole? Invent a code if he has to, but be real about it. What's with this Mr. Clean number? An altar boy whose shit doesn't smell—what'm I supposed to do with him?"

Pen was too upset, Drew decided, to hear the latest on Fraker. Today's *Wall Street Journal* had reported that Esprit, Fraker's personal computer company, had completed a second flat quarter and was close to belly-up. A massive injection of cash, an inside, unnamed source had said, was needed to mount the marketing campaign survival depended on. And cash, the article speculated, was definitely in the offing. "Once Dynagen's IPO hits the street," an industry analyst was quoted as saying, "Harriman Fraker will be able to cry all the way to the bank. And so will investors alert enough to bottom-fish Esprit."

It was easy to see what a seriously flawed IPO and a whistleblower—even a shoot-and-run whistleblower like David—would do to these hopes. And suppose word got out that two guys were nosing around Maine, trying to connect David's death with trouble at Dynagen? Suppose Cantrell, finding Drew's final remarks as provocative as he'd meant them to be, gave Fraker a call?

The Tapeworm rich was dangerous enough. Strapped and cornered, he didn't bear thinking about.

The freshman had his dorm windows open to the soft night. At this hour, the traffic that flowed down Comm. Ave. like a polluted river was thin enough to give the smells of spring half a chance against the exhaust fumes. The paper he'd just started to write was now a week late. A paper for another course was due day after tomorrow, right on top of an hour-long test in biology. He was going into the test with a D.

The princesses next door were playing Whitney Houston again. He was reaching for his own volume knob when the phone rang.

"Hi, Brad."

"Oh, no."

"You don't sound happy to hear from me. That's not nice, after all I've done for you."

"It's just that I have to study. I'm wicked far behind."

The caller clucked a disapproving tongue. "Well, the sooner we finish, the sooner you can get back to work. Got a pencil in your hand? Okay. This is a day job. Ten, ten-thirty at the latest. The quiet hour."

Brad listened, jotting notes. Midway through, grievance burst raw and sore. "You've got to be kidding. I mean, cutting that guy's tires—but you're talking heavy stuff here. I can't do it. I won't."

"Listen faggot. I know exactly what you can and can't do. Anyone who puts an innocent child's penis in his disgusting mouth—Yes. All right then. Where were we?"

Chapter 27

"Another?" Drew asked Sal Colarusso, the man he hoped would agree to head up Paladin's production and marketing.

"You swear it's harmless?"

They were drinking Armagnac. "I never said harmless. Easier on the system than cognac was all I said."

Colarusso drained his snifter. "Something tastes this good, how can it hurt?"

Drew signalled the waiter.

They were at Maison Robert, where the tables are far enough apart for privacy. Dinner had been excellent and expensive. Colarusso was an IBM star, and stars are not wooed cheaply.

Colarusso was only being prudent, he insisted. Yeah, founders' stock, yeah, enormous potential. But the good life costs. Today it costs, not just in the future.

Drew listened, once again, to the big ticket items in Colarusso's good-life inventory. The colonial on four acres in Bedford, the four-season vacation condo in New Hampshire, the four kids his wife's priest, in a just world, oughta help support, thank God Kathleen finally squared herself away on *that* bullshit.

Eyeing each other, they drank from their fresh brandies.

"I like Boone," Colarusso at length said.

"You like him as much as he likes you, can't ask for more."

"IBM, what do I say. IBM's not just security. IBM's the best."

"And you're among the best. I know it, and Boone knows it."

"Among the best? Only among?"

"Hey Sal. It's a big company."

"Yeah. Huge. Big huge Blue."

"You want that extra visibility. You want people saying Sal Colarusso put together the best operation any startup has ever been blessed with."

"More. I love it. Tell me again how it'll be down the road."

"Down the road, people will read in the paper that Paladin's astronomical growth is attributed to the talents of two visionary men, Coleman Boone and Sal Colarusso."

"Okay."

"Okay what?"

"I'm sold. You sold a master salesman. Want to know how?"

"By being right?"

"By leaving yourself off the visionary list. Even though you oughta be there."

That was Tuesday night. Alton Amy had been on the job a fruitless week. He pretended to be undiscouraged, but Drew had heard a scratch of panic in his voice. "You boys know you've got the right man on this job, don't you? Something's got to break soon, the way I'm hustling. Any day now."

"I feel like a real shit," Drew told Pen. "He wants that wheelchair so bad he can taste it. It's all I can do not to say, there, there, the check's in the mail regardless."

The medical examiner had filed a report of unattended drowning, a finding supported largely by the amount of water in David's lungs. There were no bullet or stab wounds in the body. He had recently eaten, probably a peanut butter sandwich. The blow on his forehead had not fractured the skull. The policeman who called to tell Pen this said they were closing the case.

According to Amy, news of this report had brought big relief to certain locals, proving that certain locals were keeping things under their hats. But when Drew asked for concrete evidence, Amy only repeated himself: "Everyone's acting like a load's off their backs." Drew said he'd act that way too, once he'd been assured that what had crashed into his quiet life was only an accident, not murder.

Amy would have none of this. "People here are raised to tell the truth. They're lying, it shows." But unless he got luckier, or one of his certain locals started talking, nothing was going to stop the Dynagen team from opening the road show next week.

Wednesday morning Drew had the fun of telling his partners that he'd landed Colarusso. Next he called Nanda.

"I was going to say let's get together and celebrate. But that's redundant."

Her nice giggle. "I know. Isn't it great?"

They made a plan to meet, and Drew called Coleman Boone.

"Sal Colarusso said yes, Coleman."

"Good. When can he start?"

No applause. Boone, technological genius, was innocent of production's crucial imperatives. And what was marketing? Why wouldn't Paladin just sell itself?

Drew was about to hang up when an idea struck him. "Hey Coleman? How hard is it to break in and get a record of someone's long-distance calls?"

"A smart hacker might need a day."

"Even with all the different phone companies?"

"Two days max."

"Interesting."

"You thinking of putting Paladin in people's homes?"

The earnest question jolted Drew to his senses. He'd been on the brink of asking Boone to heist the accounts of the entire Dynagen team—investment bankers, everyone. Computer invasion. An atrocity, in Boone's terms.

Drew's heart busy in his chest, he extricated himself as well as he could and hung up.

Amy had produced zilch. The long shot of having him read Irene's letters had gotten them nowhere. But so what? Boone was a man of fierce and knightly principles. Inexcusable to mess with such a man. Grotesque. Boone would have freaked out totally, never to trust Blackstone again. Rob and Sam would have Drew's ass—deservedly so. Forget that Lally had strained their confidence in his judgment. Compared to this, Lally was nothing.

If Dynagen killed David, the IPO had to be stopped. Justice required it. Drew's failure to warn David away from Morse and Cantrell required it.

And the credibility of venture capital required it. The investing public incurred risk enough when buying stock in new, essentially untried businesses. Add the taint of fraud, something wrong with MS-alpha, and the whole delicate structure starts to crumble. Then, when a good company, the kind of company he hoped Paladin would become, is ready to go public, it can't find the support it deserves.

Fraud had to be stopped. Decisively and quietly stopped, way before the starting gate. But not at any cost. Never that. He'd better watch himself.

Anticipating Nanda, springs on his feet, Drew took the long flights to his duplex two steps at a time. He was getting home later than he'd expected. Before he could turn his key, the door opened slightly. Nanda slipped through and shut it behind herself. She had a key, so he wasn't surprised to see her. But the look on her face scared him.

"Someone's been here," she whispered.

Confronted by the devastation, his first thought was a bomb. But bombs blacken, and his living room was snowy, white with feathers. Every down cushion had been slashed and flung. On the little French chairs, Granny's heavy silk upholstery had been sliced into ribbons. The tables were worse. Wood carefully tended since the eighteenth century had been cruelly and permanently crisscrossed by deep gouges.

It probably took less than fifteen minutes. There'd have been virtually no noise for neighbors to overhear.

A sheet from the memo pad he kept by his phone was propped against a lamp. NEXT IS YOUR GIRLFRIENDS' FACE, the handwritten note said. The penciled capital letters were imprecise, as if written lefty by someone right-handed. A feeble clue. The mistake in punctuation, these illiterate days, was even less useful.

The police, a detective and a patrolman, came fast but stayed forever, disbelieving nothing had been stolen. They found it incredible—all this valuable stuff lying around!—that Drew had never installed an alarm system.

The detective also had trouble believing that no one except

Miss West and the condominium manager had a key to Drew's apartment. Yes, he understood that the lock had been changed a year ago, but a year's a long time. Things get forgotten. Not by him, though. He remembered the night one of Drew's friends had tried to shoot the neighbors. Was he still seeing this woman? No? What about his current friends—any other tendencies to violence? Could someone be jealous of his relationship with Miss West?

Drew controlled himself. "No and no. Look, isn't the main issue here the threat to Nanda? And what the police can do to protect her?"

Not much, it turned out. The cruisers could keep an eye on their two houses. She shouldn't walk around alone, especially at night.

Finally they left. Nanda and Drew went slowly down the hall to his bedroom, where nothing had been disturbed.

NEXT IS YOUR GIRLFRIENDS' FACE.

She started to fold the bedspread. Neatness counts. Drew, on autopilot, helped.

For a long while they sat closely together on the edge of the bed, as bewildered as a pair of young children whose mother has just been rushed to the hospital.

"Maybe I better call," Drew finally said. "Get the detective back here, tell him about the IPO and everything."

"You're only thinking that because of me."

"Reason enough."

"No it isn't. For one thing, there's no proof this is to scare you off the IPO."

"Come on, Nanda. Why else?"

She shrugged. "Okay, forget that. The main thing is, your theories about Dynagen are just that—theories. What can you tell the police that'll serve any useful purpose? That won't set them off on rounds of questioning that could lead back to you and damage you professionally? Not to mention me?"

Her points were too good to argue against.

"Anyway," she said with a weak smile, "who's going to try anything with you around?"

Chapter 28

It hurt, Drew soon discovered, on two levels. Assault, violation, and threat blow a crater in your life. Then there's the lesser insult—the long, niggling stream of mendings, patchings, stop-payment orders. What you want is to go on a rampage or pull the covers over your head and hide. What you get is no end of opportunity to perform with diligence and conscientious care.

Shortly after eleven, the last of Drew's immediate neighbors came home for the night. For the last time, he secured the street door with the heavy slide bolt original to the house. Because of the buzzer system, this bolt was normally not used. In order to use it tonight, he'd had to play doorman four separate times. Four separate hikes up and down the stairs, four separate question-and-answer sessions with each neighbor. Fortunately only one neighbor knew the story of Maria's shootout, so, for the time being at least, there was only one reprise of the detective's suspicions.

Nothing could be done about Drew's own front door until morning. He trusted exactly one locksmith in Boston, a seasoned practitioner named Ingersoll. Over seventy, Mr. Ingersoll no longer made service calls at night.

"Let's split," Drew urgently said to Nanda. "Let's go to the Ritz."

But Nanda, chin high, wouldn't hear of it. Let the creep come back for a second round. Let him just try. She had to leave early tomorrow morning, but until then wild horses couldn't—

"What's tomorrow?" He hadn't planned on letting her out of his sight.

"Major meeting with Wink. Don't worry. I'll take a cab. Anyway, nothing's going to happen in broad daylight."

"This did."

"I mean out in the open."

She'd spoken impatiently. Don't make me more scared than I already am, he heard, and said no more.

In the morning, not long after Drew had put Nanda in her cab, Pen arrived with cameras to document the damage—to launch a second category of niggles that would wind through insurance claims, refinishers, decorator's swatch books and reupholstery. "Makes me tired just thinking about it," Drew told his cousin. "I wish my grandparents had stuck to laying up treasures in heaven."

"Mrs. Brown coming? Speaking of treasures."

"Soon as she can."

"And the fingerprint guy?"

"Sometime this morning. It's not a major priority."

"How come? Don't they have this new supercomputer that's infallible? Read about it just the other day."

"Yeah. Sherlock, it's called, which must have Conan Doyle spinning in his grave. But it only works when the criminal's prints are already on file. That's why they didn't bother dusting last night—no burglary, no burglar. The detective thinks it's some old girlfriend in a jealous frenzy."

"Creative of him."

"Forget the cops. They wrote their report, I can put in my insurance claim. What interests me is how white collar this is. If a real criminal wanted me to stop nosing around the IPO, he'd lure me into a dark alley, beat me up. Or use a gun and get rid of me altogether."

"So the slasher's an amateur?"

"No, because the lock had to be picked. But it's a coward's crime. Different from beating someone up."

"We better find out how our relevant cowards spent their time yesterday."

"What's the point? If you can hire someone to drown David you can hire a slasher."

"Maybe they're one and the same."

"Why not? Call him Joe. Amy's snooping comes to Joe's attention, Joe gets in touch with the amateur. Fits."

"Wait though. The Joe who got David had to know boats and the coast up there. This Joe had to know the city."

"So there're two Joes. Not improbable. Bad guys're thick on the ground. Like you said, read the *Globe*."

"When we were in Maine, we didn't try to keep a low profile."

"No. Not that we could have. Two look-alikes, pretty big against the sky."

"The thing is, we didn't care if we made guilty parties nervous. You were pretty damned provocative with Cantrell."

"I know, I know. And never a thought for Nanda. If anything happens to her—"

Pen gave his cousin's shoulders a crushing squeeze. "Nothing's going to happen to her. There's you and there's me. We'll stick like glue, however long it takes."

"That's the only good part. It can't take too long, assuming this is connected to the IPO. I also called in a reinforcement. Private detective named Ray Bigelow. Julia—my brief wife— stuck a tail on me once. I thought I had to stick one on her too and was lucky to find Bigelow. Damn good man. I called him right after Nanda left this morning. We're having lunch. You too, if you can get away."

Mr. Ingersoll knew locks. He also knew why Drew had needed so many changed over the years.

Now Drew's door had two locks. It was going to be a drag. Might as well live in Manhattan. "Could the guy who picked the old one pick these?"

"No lock's guaranteed against real talent. Leastways it'll take twice as long. And nothing they learn on the first one will help on the second."

"Go ahead, say it. Everyone else has."

"Say what?"

"Tell me to stop handing out keys to strange women."

"You been doing that, Mr. Lispenard?"

"A week or so ago I gave out the first key since you were here last. To a woman I hope keeps it forever."

"She's nice, huh? Young working woman? What they call a yuppie?"

"*I* wouldn't call her a yuppie. But yeah. She's young. And professional."

"Works in a nice office, right? Her own secretary and all?"

Asked what he was getting at, the locksmith produced his best seasoned-practitioner smile. Then he told Drew why this new breed of professional had become so interesting to him.

Listening, a peacock tail of spectacular possibility fanned open before Drew's eyes. Mr. Ingersoll's information, combined with Drew's earlier gleanings from his network of summer people, might very well point to nothing less than the person who had wanted David dead.

Mr. Ingersoll, in no hurry, launched into another yuppie story. But Drew was miles away, on the phone already, making his verifying calls. If he heard what he hoped to—Jesus! Talk about light at the end of the tunnel!—Alton Amy wouldn't stand a chance.

Chapter 29

Told by Drew that their deal was off otherwise, Amy had reluctantly recited the names of the Vinalhaven families he'd been watching most closely. One of the names, Arthur Sprague, had struck the bell that had brought Drew to an office in Newburyport, Massachusetts.

"You look so different. Must be the beard."

"The beard and seventeen years," said Drew.

The woman with the sleek blond hair smiled. "You didn't stroke it. Usually men can't discuss their beards without stroking them."

"What about it, Willow?"

"Hm?"

"Are you going to call Arthur now or five minutes from now?"

She picked up a pencil and tapped it lightly on the blotter of her desk. Her nails, which Drew remembered being broken and bitten, were long. Their polish matched the apricot silk of her blouse. More apricot, faintly iridescent, shone on her lips.

"Can't I sleep on it? Or at least eat on it?"

"When I called I offered dinner. You said you'd rather see me in your office. So. Now or five minutes from now?"

An ingenuous smile. "I got you here to impress you."

"It worked. I'm knocked out. The mahogany. The view of the harbor. The signed lithographs. The Oriental."

"Small but real," she said of the carpet. "Shiraz."

"And you yourself, looking terrific. Of course, you always did. You were the best-looking sternman Camden, Maine, ever saw. No wonder Arthur fell for you."

She gestured at the view. "Newburyport reminds me of Camden. Not enough, but somewhat."

Willoughby Barns was a Vice-President in a development company that specialized in turning old port cities into tourist attractions. They'd started with a tiny piece of the new Baltimore, she'd told Drew proudly, then gone on to Portland, Maine, and now, home base in Newburyport.

Drew hitched his chair closer to her desk. "Of course, a big job like yours, you have to look good. You need a nice smile, for example."

Willow started to run her tongue over her front teeth, caught herself, and looked unhappy.

When she and Drew met, she was on the verge of having a number of these pretty teeth pulled. It was the summer before Drew started college. He was cruising around Maine with a school friend named Hicks Mallory in Hicks's father's yawl. Willow was twenty-four, an older woman and latter-day hippie. Her pursuit of the nonmaterialistic life, coupled with carelessness, had landed her with a mouthful of constant pain. On board the yawl were abundant supplies of marijuana and vodka. Willow would drop by after lobstering to dose herself. Drew, whose senior-year English course had included Eugene O'Neill, was worried enough about addiction to drag her to a decent dentist. The estimate for the root canals, caps, and crowns she needed astonished him, but he wrote out the zeros and signed the check with, he believed, an air of sophisticated ease.

"I'm calling a debt, that's all," he now told her.

"Damn you."

Drew shrugged.

"It's not fair. Not a word for years and now this. How'd you find me, anyway?"

"I remembered you came from a town on Long Island with an Indian name. Ma something. I looked at a road map and found Mattatuck, Mastic, Manhasset, and Massapequa. My secretary and I called all the Barneses with an E. Then without an E. Then I found your mother in Massapequa. She was very communicative."

Willow's expression confirmed Drew's guess that mother and daughter weren't friends. "A debt," he said again.

"He'll hate me."

"Chalk it up to interest. Or inflation."

"What a mean cold bastard you are. Always were. You should see yourself. You look like a hatchet."

She'd said something similar that summer when, for reasons he still didn't understand, Drew turned down her proposed barter of sex for dentistry. Furious, she'd gone after Hicks, so showily and incessantly that Drew decided to quit the cruise and spend the rest of his vacation in Brookline with his aunt and uncle. Whether or not Willow ever actually made it with Arthur remained a mystery. The two of them acted like spoony kids together, so tenderly blissed out you had to wonder how they summoned the energy to haul the heavy traps. When Arthur took up with Willow, his entire family, wife, children, grandchildren, stopped speaking to him. He was too lovestruck to care.

The last Drew heard from Hicks, was that Willow was going to UMass Boston. She'd left Arthur because she loved him too much to deny him a dignified old age with his family. That had been, what, fifteen years ago, the whole story forgotten until Amy, mercilessly pressed, had delivered his name.

"Pick up the phone, Willow."

Arthur Sprague, formerly of Camden, now the resident of a house trailer parked on his daughter's Vinalhaven property, answered on the second ring.

"Hang on just a sec, Arthur." She covered the mouthpiece. "Out. I'm not talking with you listening."

When she opened the door, her eyes were red and her makeup streaked. "That was awful. *Awful.*"

"I know. I'm sorry."

"You don't know anything. You didn't hear him. The hurt in his voice. A decent old man—I made him break his *code.*"

"Just tell me what he said and I'll get out of your life forever."

"There's a Stonington family named Richardson. Father used to fish, but he's home with a bad heart. The mother picks crab. There's a daughter, Doreen, who's a nurse at Penobscot Memorial. One son, Clayton, is a marine. Stationed in California, Arthur thinks. He's an Agent Orange victim and can't have kids. You don't like this little tale. Good. Suffer, if you're capable of it. The other son moved to Portland and bought himself a nearly new fishing boat. The *Betty Ann*. No one knows where he got the money. Arthur saw the *Betty Ann* off Calderwood Island on April sixteenth. He remembers because he'd been out netting shrimp for his grandson's birthday party.''

''Did he actually see Richardson?''

''What? Sure.''

''He said he saw him.''

''I don't know. I think so. I'm not calling back, so don't bother asking. You can pull my teeth out one by one. Enough's enough.''

Drew agreed. He felt bad about Arthur. He'd started feeling bad right after Amy had said there was one old coot in particular who'd been acting funny. ''Silly old coot name of Sprague,'' he'd gone on. ''Made a fool of himself over a young girl once. Tongues wagging up and down the bay.''

''I'm grateful, Willow.''

''Fuck you.''

Nothing worth saying, he took himself and the bad taste in his mouth out of there. A man's code was a serious matter. He'd made Willow do to Arthur Sprague what he himself had narrowly escaped doing to Coleman Boone.

Dan Richardson. Dan Richardson killed David Benoit.

Prying loose Richardson's name had cost three innocent bystanders more than they'd wanted to pay. But the rest, so far, was only cheap words.

Long night ahead. Lots of sociable phone gossip with his network of summer people.

Gossip, Drew knew, was the lifeblood of this tribe, solidifying its members' sense of specialness and exclusivity. Which was nothing to get snooty about. If not for their snug little, smug little world, their incessant need to keep track of the smallest details of one another's lives, there'd be no hope that Richardson's name might spark the right connection. Solder the link that would justify its high cost.

Chapter 30

Friday, while Drew was trying to focus on Blackstone's weekly meeting, copies of Dynagen's final prospectus reached the eager hands of the investment community. The substitution of Virginia Carmichael's name for David's had caused only a week's delay, a reflection of Washington's confidence in Norris, Pitney, the chief underwriter.

The final price was a rich twenty-five dollars per share. Excitement was intense. A customer warned by his or her broker that an order for a thousand shares might not be filled was apt to start begging for fifteen hundred. The more remote the odds, the more insistently rang the phones. Brokers dangled an astonishing variety of bait—You want my boat this August? Season tickets? My girlfriend's a model, how about her?—in the hope of increasing their allotments.

By Saturday morning, Mrs. Brown had pounced on the last stray feather and sent the furniture into storage.

"More?" Drew asked Nanda, lifting the coffee pot.

"God no. I'm so wired I'll bounce off the ceiling."

She had an odd look on her face. He told her so.

"I keep wondering who's the handsome stranger. You going to grow it back?"

He'd shaved. If Richardson was their man, the beard might tip him off. "Probably."

"Good. I think. You *do* look handsome."

The buzzer sounded. Geoff, come to pick her up and take her to safety in Newton. Drew's idea. "When you're out on the firing line?" she'd cried. "Forget it." They'd fought. Drew had won.

Drew and Geoff shook hands. A quick sizing up. Nanda had to laugh. "Men," she told the ceiling. But she kissed Drew full on the mouth anyway. So there. Then she became as fierce as she felt. "If you don't take care of yourself," she warned, "I'll make you even sorrier."

The cousins took Pen's unremarkable Ford and cellular phone. Ray Bigelow might need to call them during their drive to Portland. And no telling how many other ways a car phone might come in handy.

Bigelow had been keeping track of Richardson since Thursday night, having left for Portland right after Drew called him from Newburyport. So far, except for a pizza run late Friday night, Richardson hadn't strayed from home—the rented ground floor of a shabby two-family house.

"Bigelow's all right," said Pen.

"But?"

"I could do it better."

"Absolutely. Question of disguise, though. Have to shrink you and so forth."

They'd been over this ground before, lengthily. As before, Drew stuck to what was undeniable. Since the appearance of two look-alikes, shaved beard notwithstanding, could be fatal, one of the cousins had to stay hidden. And since he alone had sufficient fluency in finance to bait the trap without misstep or hesitation, the hidden cousin had to be Pen.

Pen, wrathful, pronounced him one fucking stubborn dude. A label Drew was happy to paste all over himself. Anything to keep Pen sidelined. Anything to fend off macho notions of what a real man would do, whether or not anyone, himself included, could count on him to keep his cool.

The *Betty Ann*'s berth was close in. Drew and Bigelow would start at the far end of the fish pier.

Everything about Bigelow was medium—build, height, brownness and thinness of hair, length of nose, strength of chin, depth of blue in the eyes. Medium and forgettable, Drew realized—valuable for his line of work. The glen plaid suit, medium gray, wouldn't fool Wall Street, but Maine was a long way from finicky urban distinctions. Anyway, let's hear it for polyester. How else can you look spruce after a couple of days on stakeout?

The wind sliced off water the color of oiled steel and cut through their clothes. The low sun was invisible behind thick gray clouds. Grit and fast-food wrappings blew restlessly around.

This late Saturday, most of the fleet was in, with skippers home for the night. To the few men still working on board, Drew and Bigelow, wearing coats and ties, were conspicuous. "Thought you was looking to charter," one, a ruddy-faced giant, said.

By the time they reached the *Betty Ann*, dusk had fallen. Richardson was bent over his trawling lines, fiddling in a make-work way. A roll of flesh, lard white, showed between his sweatshirt and belt. He's waiting for us, Drew thought. He's no less curious than the others about what two city guys are doing here on a cold Saturday.

Not your basic hardscrabble tub, the *Betty Ann*. Lines lay neatly coiled in their tubs, hooks free of rust. The decks shone with unblemished paint. The windows had been cleaned of salt spray.

"Pretty safe bet the drug boys helped him buy it," Bigelow said in an undertone. "That radar and VHF? Top of the line. Tail a man for days with those babies."

All at once Drew saw David—trimming sail, minding wind and water, never once suspecting every move was being stalked. The image braced him. Exactly what he needed.

"Nice boat," called Bigelow.

Richardson straightened up. Coors baseball cap pulled low, lank dark hair, jeans with a greasy sheen. The gray hooded sweatshirt had dirty cuffs. An ex-weightlifter, Drew decided. The big shoulders were round, nothing holding them up.

"Got a minute?" Bigelow said, his voice rich with good fellowship.

Richardson shrugged.

"Okay if we hop aboard?"

"I guess."

"I'm Ray Bigelow and this is Sam Kent. You're? Hey, Dan,

nice to meet you. Sam and I grew up together, over near Augusta. Moved to Boston around the same time. I'm in real estate, he's in the money game."

"New businesses," Drew amplified. "It works like this. A man comes to me with a bright idea. I like it, I give him some money to start the ball rolling."

Bigelow winked. "Takes his little cut, Sam does. Sixty, seventy percent."

"Damn straight I take a cut. Anyone wants charity, they can go to the government."

Richardson liked this. Under that beer bloat, a shred of normal downeast righteousness.

"Well anyway," Drew continued. "The other day this guy comes in. Fisherman out of Gloucester, Mass. He's fed up trying to compete with the Russians and their big factory ships. What he wants to do is build an American fleet, same size. Beat the bastards at their own game."

Bigelow cut in. "Sam thinks it's a terrific idea. Calls me up, offers me a chance to share the wealth. Better check it out, I say. Talk to the guys in the trenches. So here we are, Dan. Factory ships, Americanski style. How's it sound to you? See any problems?"

Richardson hitched his jeans and spat overboard. "Crew."

"What about crew?" Drew asked.

"Those Russkies're cooped up like monkeys in cages. No white man's gonna stand for that. Which leaves niggers. Niggers're crazy for fishing. Drive across any river, there they are. But the ocean? Forget it. Niggers gotta have their feet on the ground. Plus, they can't take the cold."

Bigelow chortled and punched Drew's arm. "Pay up, my man. One hundred percent negative on your Americanski fleet."

Drew, disgusted, pulled out his wallet and found a crisp fifty.

Bigelow snatched at it and moved a confiding step closer to Richardson. "The trouble with guys like Sam here is they spend all their time on the fiftieth floor of some skyscraper. Can't even open their windows. No, I'm serious. The windows on lots of those big buildings are totally sealed. No wonder they lose touch with basic reality, right?"

"Cities suck," Richardson agreed.

Drew shrugged. "I get by. There're certain compensations."

Bigelow flourished the fifty. "Hey, Dan. You won a bet for me, the least I can do is buy you a drink. I know me and Sam're ready—this talking's thirsty work. Didn't I see a place a couple blocks back? Glad to give you a lift—okay, fine, we'll follow you."

Chapter 31

The Harborview was a neighborhood joint, untouched by the gentrification that developers like Willow had brought to downtown Portland. A stale eternity of cigarette and cigar smoke mixed with exhalations of pine soap and piss from the men's room. An enormous color TV blared from a high corner shelf. Five men in work clothes had spaced themselves along the bar to nurse drinks and watch the ballgame. When the three newcomers entered, all five minded their own business. The bartender too. If anyone here knew Richardson, he wasn't letting on.

"Fucking Mets," Bigelow said, steering Richardson to one of the small tables ranged against the wall. "No offense, Dan?"

"Shit no. I hate them."

Sports talk took them through the first round. Midway through the second, they moved back to the fucking Russkies. "And don't forget," Richardson reminded them, "the Canadians screwed us right out of the processing market. Guys like me cut off at the knees. Not that anyone gives a fuck. Government treats us like fucking robots."

"Robots!" cried Bigelow. "There's your answer, Sam. A factory ship with robots."

"Know how to tell a robot from a Russkie?" Richardson cracked. "Can't be done."

Everyone laughed. Drew went to the bar to pick up the next round. When he came back, the other two were still laughing. "We've got it, Sam. Clones. Dan's gonna sneak out to Georges Banks and snatch a Russkie. We take him to that biotech outfit of yours and you clone us up a whole crew. You make them Russkie enough to live like animals but totally loyal to the U.S. of A.''

"Very funny. But I think my biotech outfit, as you call it, has enough on its plate already.''

"Like?''

"Little things like a miracle cure. How does fifty for one grab you?''

"What fifty for one. Fifty for one *what*?''

"Dollars, Ray, dollars. Starting next week, every buck I put into Dynagen gives me back fifty.''

"Jesus Christ.''

"Yup. Took just a tad more than a year.''

"I don't believe this. Fifty for one. It's indecent.''

"Hey. I'm hurting, next to the founders. The original bright-idea boys. They never put in a penny and they're making out like bandits. Couple million for Dr. Larry, couple million for Dr. Wade. Not bad, huh? Dan, maybe you saw Dr. Wade on the Donahue show.''

"Huh?''

"Phil Donahue? Dr. Wade Cantrell?''

"Never watch it.''

"Well, Ray here saw it all right. Ray's been pestering me ever since, looking for a piece of the action.''

"And you keep bragging how long a line I have to stand in.''

"It's long, all right. Ask Harriman Fraker. Ask Nat Partridge.''

Bigelow rolled his eyes. "What're these guys, famous or something? I'm supposed to know them? Wait. How many pigs're at this trough, anyway?''

"Fraker and Partridge are investors. Big investors. They put in a million each.''

"Jesus. They get fifty million back? Both of them?''

"Yup. And Mr. Partridge gets even more. Two years back, he put in five hundred thou. The way it works—it's complicated—early money's worth more. An *extra* fifty million, close to.''

"Unbelievable. You believe this, Dan?''

Richardson, noticeably dazed, shook his head and drank.

Bigelow radiated resentment. "There's no justice, am I right? I mean, take fishing. You put yourself right on the line—squalls, big seas, what have you. Sweat in summer, freeze in winter. Risk your neck three hundred sixty-five days a year. And then who makes out?"

"Not me. Guarantee you that."

"And what about the food processors? Mrs. Whoosie's Fish Cakes, that crowd. What pisses me off, none of them would have a thing to do in their damn skyscrapers if men like you, Dan, didn't supply the raw material. The basic commodity, know what I'm saying? You're it, right? The whole entire structure relies on you to produce the basic commodity. But do you get fifty for one? Huh?"

"It's the whole fucking system," cried Richardson. "Man tries to get out, they got him by the balls."

"Just a second," Drew said. "Don't think the money game's all roses. I take risks too. Plenty of risks. Plus, you're fishing, you're your own boss. That can be pretty nice. I mentioned Nat Partridge before? He's got these partners. One's this incredible skinflint. Charlie Hammond. He'll negotiate an hour to squeeze an extra buck out of a deal. And Wink Halsey. Wink. What kind of name is that for a grown man? Least you're your own boss, Dan."

"Better believe it."

"Goes a long way, take it from me."

"Back up, Sam. Back up to risks. This Dynagen deal got any risks? I mean, here I am, busting my nuts to get a piece."

"Of course there's risk. All down the line. Regulatory, production, you name it. But unless something goes wrong in the next couple days, knock wood, we're home free."

"Seriously? That close and it's still chancy?"

Simplifying greatly, Drew explained the mechanism and timing of the IPO. "Monday morning they go out to California to talk the company up," he concluded. "Should be no sweat, because multiple sclerosis is such a terrible disease, right? Now all you have to worry about is one of the doctors, God forbid, smashing himself up in a car wreck. So much dough riding on the brains of a couple of men—that's what I call risk." He was very grave. "Mortal men," he reminded them.

Bigelow, too, was overwhelmed. "All those millions out of one little idea."

Richardson spit some air through his teeth and gave his empty beer bottle a vicious spin.

Bigelow waited to see if he'd say something. Then he checked his watch. "Hey Sam. Time's flying." He leered at Richardson. "We've got ladies waiting. Mine's a redhead, know what I mean? Besides, I better get this one out of here before he starts saying it's harder to make Mrs. Whoosie's Fish Cakes than run a trawler out of Casco Bay."

"He's kidding, Dan. Tell the man you're kidding, Ray."

"It's true. I'm kidding."

"I may be out of touch but I'm not out of my mind. Nice talking to you, Dan."

"Yeah. Same here."

"Have a good one, Dan. See you again sometime."

"Went okay," Bigelow said when they were safe inside Pen's car.

"Think he's hooked?"

"I do. Couple of times I was scared he'd spot the hook. Why I swung into my Joe Jokester routine."

"What do you say about a guy like that?"

"Piece of shit. Why? You feel bad for setting him up?"

"It's more like I feel bad, period."

"Well. This stuff's new for you."

"What about when he said the system gets you by the balls?"

"Yeah. Bet anything he hired out as a killer to buy his life back from some drug wholesaler. Shows how stupid he is. They don't let their errand boys loose, as a rule. You do one run, you've got yourself a new career. For life. Try to get loose, they give you a short life."

A gigantic yawn shook Drew's whole frame. "You done good in there, Ray."

"Done good yourself, Sam."

Pleased and surprised by the compliment—Bigelow was so tough and self-contained he hadn't even yawned in sympathy—Drew started the car and headed for Richardson's street and Pen.

Chapter 32

The animal stood erect, hind claws dug in, forepaws flailing like a panicked swimmer. Richardson knew he had to stop thinking about the money. He had to cool out, clear his head.

He dropped into his La-Z-Boy and loosened his belt. Using remote, he switched on the TV.

The movie, long in progress, had that actor who looks like Lee Marvin. Richardson could never remember his name. Usually he played tough guys, but this time he had a hospital job. Mr. PacMan, they called him. PacMan. Anyone play that anymore? If he had a nickel for every quarter—

Money again. Everywhere you fucking turn.

The movie. What was going on? Mr. PacMan's classy girlfriend wanted to drive him to California. Made sense—the town they lived in looked worse than Portland in February. So why didn't they up and go? And who's this other girlfriend? A slut. Never out of her bathrobe. Great bod, but a slut.

The longer Richardson watched, the more opaque the story became. He flicked around the dial. The animal rampaged in his gut. The money. The millions. Fifty for one.

With a yell of despair he found the movie again and cut the sound. Mr. PacMan silently called his cat down from the roof. He took the cat inside, up to his room. He kissed it and hugged it, taking his time. Then he opened his medicine cabinet. It was full of different kinds of dope. Stuff he'd lifted from the hospital, Richardson bet. Very slowly and gently, Mr. PacMan prepared a needle and injected the cat.

The whole long drawn-out scene was so loving, so suggestively peaceful, that the animal quieted too. Richardson slid into sleep, the movie ending without him.

He awoke with his tongue stuck sourly to the rest of his

mouth and a painful crick in his neck. The TV was blank. Night or morning? He squinted at his watch. Four thirty.

His animal lay still. The millions, he tested. Not a stir. He tried again: fifty for one. Still nothing.

If he started now he'd be there before seven. Haul the fucker right out of bed. Bust his door down, haul him right out. Watch that big-time look fade fast. Watch the wife, hair twisted into curlers, dive under the covers.

The scene, vivid, archetypal, stroked Richardson as he drove south. Over and over again he saw the wife sit bolt upright, covers at her skinny chest, eyes popping with fear. Over and over her mouth widened into a huge terrified hole.

Just before he crossed the Massachusetts line his animal shifted position. Richardson loosened his belt and pants. A lazy, stretching scrape. Then nothing.

The money, he tested. Still nothing. The animal wanted him to go for it.

Maintaining an undetectable tail on a long stretch of highway presents problems. Bigelow's method for hours of thin traffic was to sandwich the pursued, turning him into an unwitting pursuer of a lead car. The tail could then stay mostly out of sight behind both of them.

Even with phones, driving lead took the most finesse. And much as Bigelow had respected Drew's performance in the Harborview, he was glad that the cousins would take the simpler job of invisible rear sweep.

Drew himself had settled the question. "We can sit low," he said, "but we can't sit narrow. Richardson's not the brightest, but he's bound to think he's seen shoulders like that someplace before."

"He'll go apeshit when he finds you here," Geoff West told his sister.

"Will you shut up on that? Please?"

Nanda was supposed to wait in the car. Instead she'd claimed the vantage offered by the recessed doorway of the brownstone. Overgrown rhododendrons filled the postage-stamp front yard. In relative comfort, she could see without being seen. Geoff had to hunker down behind the bushes.

The brownstone was empty, in the process of being rehabbed into condos. On a Sunday, no workmen would be around to interfere. It was six thirty. The sun wouldn't be warm for hours. Nanda hugged herself and wished she'd thought to bring her down parka. Nothing like down for security.

A dozen sparrows argued territory in the tall elm whose roots humped the bricks of the sidewalk. A pair of joggers, a gay couple Nanda knew by sight, passed on their way to the Esplanade—the only people she'd seen this morning. They wore matching outfits, beards and haircuts. Their strides matched too, and with good reason. Both sets of earphones were tethered to a single Walkman.

Definitely not the same kind of gay as Pen and David, she decided. But which was the dominant partner? The guy who carried the cassette called the tune, set the pace. On the other hand, this, and all other schlepping, might fall to the submissive one.

Dominant, submissive, what was wrong with her? She'd have a fit if someone tried to pin labels like that on her. And a bigger fit if Drew got mad at her for moving in close, acting like a normal red-blooded human being.

Chunky man, baseball cap. Pounding up the walkway. Punching the doorbell again again again.

Everything flattened, became a movie. The door opened. The man was pulled inside. A car drove up and parked across the street, then another. From the first car two men came running, making straight for Nanda's hiding place.

The movie stopped. Nanda was in Drew's arms, babbling. Yes, yanked him right in, not a word, definitely not. No hesitation whatsoever.

"How're you doing?" Pen asked his old teammate.

"Great," said Geoff, too excited to remember that more than fun was happening here.

By grabbing the step railing of the brownstone and leaning out, you could see a wedge of bow-fronted library—a reading lamp, the back of a big leather chair, bookshelves filled with leather-bound sets. The glass was alarmed. They couldn't break in without alerting the police, blowing their carefully set trap.

"I'm going for a closer look," said Pen.

He climbed over the railing and dropped lightly onto the ivy that filled the neat little yard. Planting his big hands on the library sill, he hoisted himself up.

Nothing. Moving quickly, he gave the door a try. Locked. He cupped his ear. Still nothing.

"They built solid in those days," he said when he came back to the brownstone. "Guess you're on, Geoff."

Delighted, Geoff streaked for Bigelow's car. Late Thursday night, long after Drew finished chatting with his summer people, he and Nanda had scouted the scene. Super sneaky, they'd used Nanda's bike. Like most Back Bay houses, this one had a walled garden off the service alley. Nanda held the bike steady against the wall and Drew climbed up, balancing on its seat. Opening onto the garden was a kitchen with sliding glass doors. These were alarmed, but not the wall itself—he'd have set it off.

Geoff, the only one nobody inside would recognize, would get a boost from Bigelow and scale the wall.

The front door banged open. Bat out of hell, Richardson took the steps at a bound. Halfway to his car, he ran smack into Pen's right fist.

Drew had finally agreed that Pen could do whatever he had to as long as there was no serious noise and no one was around to see.

Seconds later, Bigelow pulled up and jumped out. "He dead yet?"

"Just sleeping," said Pen.

They got Richardson into the back seat and drove him to his Toyota. The joggers Nanda had seen earlier rounded the corner. Waiting for them to pass, Pen dug for and found Richardson's car keys. The transfer was speedy and, as far as they knew, unwitnessed. Bigelow, taking no chances, split. He intended to tip 911—guy in car, Maine plates, looks half dead—anonymously and from a distance.

Pen loped off toward Boylston, stuffing his identifying sweater in a dumpster along the way. Just in case. Two blocks upwind from the beating he would turn back into the residential area and, at walking pace, join the others.

His hands were numb, the wrists ominously buzzing. That last kick had pulled something in his groin. He felt more than equal to what lay ahead. Terrific, in fact.

Chapter 33

Banging out, Richardson had left the door of the house wide open. Drew turned to Nanda. "Shall we?"

"Oh Lord."

"You don't have to."

"Yes I do."

Geoff was at the garden doors, waiting for them. Drew let him in and they exchanged a few quick words. Geoff nodded and left for his car.

Nat Partridge, in pajamas and robe, lay as if flung. Blood ran from his nose and a cut lip. His face was frighteningly gray. The last time Drew had seen human flesh that color he'd been standing in Vernon Cardwell's undertaking parlor.

But Partridge wasn't dead. Wincing, he slowly raised himself until he sat, his back against the kitchen cabinets. He accepted without comment the wad of wet paper towel Nanda held out to him. Carefully he mopped at eyes, nose, and mouth, stopping to stare amazed at the redness and quantity of his blood.

"What the hell," he began, but the effort of this bluster started his coughing. "—doing in my house?" he feebly finished.

"Richardson left the door open," said Drew. "We thought you might need a doctor."

"No doctor."

"Just to check the ribs?"

"I said no."

"I'll get some ice for that eye," said Nanda.

"No ice. Just go away and leave me alone."

"Sorry," said Drew. "Can't do that, Nat."

"Are your sons good sleepers?" Nanda asked.

Her question had a reviving effect on the man. "It's spring vacation. My wife has taken the boys to visit their grandmother."

"Lucky break," said Drew, meaning it for himself as well. This was going to be hard enough without adding innocents. "Let's get you off the floor."

Partridge not protesting, Drew and Nanda eased him into one of the Windsor chairs that circled a handsome old cherry table. Nanda, Drew saw, was hanging by a thread. And Pen should arrive any minute now. Better go for quick and dirty.

He smiled encouragingly at Partridge. "How did you get him to do it?"

"How did I get whom to do what?"

"Dan Richardson to kill David Benoit."

"Richardson?"

"The same Richardson who just beat you up."

Partridge was all craft. "You know that man? How extraordinary. I never saw him before in my life."

"Cut it out, Nat." Nanda's voice was ashy. "You practically dragged him into your house. I was watching from next door."

A flicker of cold rage. "Really. Your word against mine, of course."

Drew suddenly sat tall, ready to lunge and bite. "Listen up, Nat. Listen carefully. Richardson came here to get money—a cut of the Dynagen millions. We know because we set him up. Our man out there heard him say he killed for you. At the time he was kicking your guts in. If our man hadn't banged on the window he might've killed you too. You getting this, Nat? We know everything. In a few minutes I'm going to pick up the phone and call an emergency meeting—Cantrell, Morse, Fraker, Peale, Hammond, and Halsey. There isn't going to be any IPO. Hear me? No IPO."

"Indeed."

Drew went lazy, let the silence build.

Nat's hands, hurt and cradled in his lap, were shaking. Without this tiny sign of humanity, Nanda might start screaming and never stop.

"This is some kitchen, Nat," Drew lazily observed. "Beautiful cabinetwork. Beautiful house, what I saw of it. Makes me wonder about you, though. Man has everything money can buy, why's he kill to get more?"

Pen stood in the doorway.

A strange gargle from Partridge. His eyes swiveled from one cousin to the other. Finally he settled on Drew, demanding his name.

Nanda caught on first. "That's Drew. He shaved his beard."

Partridge couldn't take it in. Until this moment, he'd assumed he was dealing with Drew's fag cousin, David Benoit's fag boyfriend. But this was something the others didn't figure out until later. What they saw now was collapse and, for the first time, fear.

Pen joined them at the table and Drew bore down. "We were discussing money, Pen. I was about to observe that there are many things in life, desirable things, that money can't buy. It's sad, isn't it, Nat? No IPO, no more cheers from the boys at the backgammon table. No more pats on the back from Charlie Tucker. Back to the bad old days of zero respect."

A look of pure hate before Partridge could shake off the goad. "Breaks of the game," he mumbled. "Win some, lose some."

Pen spoke. "You ask this dirtbag why he didn't pay up? Save himself a beating?"

"Not yet. How about it, Nat?"

Partridge was rallying. Every inch the wintry aristocrat, he didn't deign to answer.

"I guess you put two and two together," Drew said, as if sympathetically. "Richardson shows up, you knew someone had talked to him. Someone who was onto the scam at Dynagen. You'd be throwing good money after bad, so to speak. Besides, Richardson's such a ruffian. A gentleman doesn't allow a ruffian to call the shots. Especially someone who used to be your yard boy."

The sucker punch. Partridge's little rally was history.

"We better start calling people about the meeting," Nanda said.

"Upsie daisy, Nat," said Pen.

A cousin on each side, he was escorted upstairs to dress.

Chapter 34

Weird, Drew thought, looking around Blackstone's conference table. Something out of place.

Then he had it. The men had arrived in weekend clothes—chinos, knit shirts, elderly blazers. The set and actors were familiar, the costumes not—except in Morse's case. He was togged out in the same thrift-shop pants and stained white lab coat he always wore.

Hammond, Halsey, and Peale looked worried. Fraker, Morse, and Cantrell were affronted. Royally pissed.

Morse had slung a leg over the arm of his chair and was popping his knuckles like a lout of fifteen. The pained forbearance Cantrell had wrapped himself in kept splitting seams, revealing rage beneath. Fraker—Drew was sorry all over again he hadn't turned out to be the murderer—drummed the table and smoked.

"It's after ten," he said. "Let's start."

Charlie Hammond frowned. "Shouldn't we wait for Nat?"

Drew and Nanda had left Partridge guarded by Pen and Geoff. "He had the same invitation as everyone else," Nanda gently reminded her boss.

"What about Louis Ralli?" Fraker demanded. "What about Victor Chu? Why isn't the whole board here?"

"We thought a smaller meeting was best," Drew told him.

"Yeah? Who's we?"

"Myself, Nanda West, and Pen Mauran. My cousin. When Nat decides to join us, Pen will bring him."

"Oh dear," said Cantrell.

Drew ignored him. "The three of us believe that David Benoit was killed by a man named Dan Richardson. We believe that Richardson was acting for Nat Partridge."

158

"You believe." Fraker sneered it. "Who cares what you believe. What can you prove?"

"I'll get to that. First I want you all to know that my original involvement had absolutely nothing to do with Dynagen. Neither did Nanda's. Our ties to David Benoit were entirely personal—through my cousin Pen."

Cantrell's eyebrows insinuated.

"Good man, Pen." Peale said this so decisively no one wondered how he knew.

Drew gave Peale a nod and launched into a highly simplified summary. "Pen was the first of us to reject the idea that David's drowning was accidental. Guy was born determined. He also knows the coast of Maine like I know my desktop. He produced Richardson and Richardson led us to Nat."

"And you're positive," Wink Halsey asked, "that Nat knew this Richardson?"

He sounded plaintive. Maybe it was all a bad dream.

"He knew him," said Nanda.

"But he admits nothing?"

"Complete stonewall."

"Damn the man! Why isn't he here?"

Instead of dumping everything on us, Wink meant. Nanda, pure impulse, patted his arm.

Taking some typed pages from the folder in front of him, Drew passed copies around. "I hope someone will tell me what this is," he said.

Peale took a look and showed surprise. "Isn't it a capsule operating budget?"

Cantrell looked straight at Nanda. "Where did you get this? This is highly confidential information."

Drew had been gambling. Now relief hit him like a swallow of good brandy. "It's Dynagen's budget, then. Good." He passed around another set of pages. "I xeroxed this from an envelope that was in David's suit pocket—the suit he wore his last day at work.

"You can see what I did—took the numbers jotted on the envelope and typed them in standard budget format. I'd guess that the bottom line on the right is what David thought Dynagen would need to operate for another year if the IPO was postponed. Wade, Larry, do either of you remember seeing David jot on an envelope that morning? Well, doesn't matter. The point is, he needed to figure, as any conscientious financial officer would, how to carry on without the IPO revenue.''

Peale, Drew saw, was beginning to understand. The only one so far, but then Peale had been David's friend. Who'd catch on last? Fraker? Cantrell?

Wait, though. Cantrell had to be paid back for accusing Nanda of espionage. ''Knowing David, Wade, these projections are probably sound. Having them worked out like this should mean real time savings for you when you cancel the IPO, start picking up the pieces.''

''Now just a minute,'' Cantrell exploded. ''Whoa way back. No one's canceling anything. Dynagen belongs to me—to myself and Larry. We've knocked ourselves out, body and soul. No one's going to take what's rightfully ours.''

''Dynagen isn't yours,'' snapped Fraker. ''Some of it's mine and some's Hammond, Halsey's. But for Jesus's sweet sake, Lispenard! Cut the cute conjecture and give it to us straight.''

''I wasn't there Tuesday morning. Cute conjecture's the best I can manage.''

''Wade.'' Hammond had his gloves off. ''Tell us what happened Tuesday.''

A heavy sigh. ''David had a bee in his bonnet about the IPO. He insisted we postpone it. Nat lectured him on the closing window and all, but he paid no attention. Then he stomped out and didn't come back. I'm sorry he's dead. Real sorry. But I'm sure as hell not sorry he can't wreck the offering.''

Fraker was beside himself. ''Postpone? Why the fuck were you talking postponement?''

Shit, thought Drew. He's innocent all around.

Neither doctor would speak.

''Wade,'' Hammond ordered.

Heartstopping loud in the dead silence, the telephone rang. Nanda, closest, swiveled her chair to answer it.

''Oh no,'' she wailed.

And listened a minute longer. ''Right. Right. Sure.''

''It's horrible,'' she told the men in the room. ''Nat has killed himself.''

Chapter 35

Everyone talking at once, it took a while for Nanda to tell the little she knew. Nat had said he was ready to confront his associates, but first he needed to pick up some papers in his office. Somehow—Pen would explain, he was talking to the police right now—Nat had distracted his keepers long enough to bash a hole in the window and dive to his death.

"I thought this cousin of yours knew what he was doing," Fraker said.

Crime of passion, Drew thought for an icy moment. Irrational loss of control.

Nanda's chin lifted. "Pen has been totally reliable throughout this whole nasty business. Totally."

"No more fencing, Harriman," Hammond said in a tone of tired but final authority. "Wade and Larry have something to tell us."

Morse unhooked his leg and slapped an exasperated palm against the table. "Benoit stuck his nose in where it didn't belong. Shut up, Wade, I'm telling this my way. The monoclonal worked for eight months. Then this meningitis reaction set in. No big deal. All I had to do was adjust the monoclonal. But that wasn't enough for Benoit."

As abruptly as he'd begun, Morse stopped. He'd told everything there was to tell. Time to go home.

Hammond's handsome Yankee face blazed red. "Is that all you have to say for yourself? After sitting on this thing for nearly a month? What's going on? What's the status of MS-alpha?"

"I'm recoding it. Doing exactly what I told Benoit I was going to. Nothing more or less."

"May I, Larry? Gentlemen?" Dynagen's Great Communicator was about to burst. "A little biology may help. MS-alpha, you'll remember, is a monoclonal antibody. Like every other monoclonal, it's foreign to the host. It has to be disguised—coded—in such a way that the host won't reject it and prevent its free movement through the bloodstream."

He swept the table with a confident smile. "MS-alpha performed brilliantly for a period considerably longer than conservative laboratory standards. When the viral side effect emerged, almost certainly a result of the original coding, there was no reason for alarm. David Benoit was completely out of line."

"I don't buy that," said Peale. "The stock issue's claim to fame is the product. We're selling a miracle cure in hand, not in the bush."

"With all due respect, Chris, you lack the scientific capacity to make that distinction."

"Really. Are you prepared to guarantee a schedule? Or the effectiveness of the recoding? And what happens if the new one brings on some other—what did you call it? Viral side effect? Polio, for instance?"

"Or AIDS," said Wink Halsey. "That's a virus too."

"Again, these are lay questions. Larry and I are fully prepared to guarantee a properly coded monoclonal. We can also guarantee no one in the world is anywhere near us." He smiled. "Of course, the sooner we get back to our labs, the better."

Drew couldn't take much more of this. "When David turned up missing, Wade, what did you think?"

Caught by surprise, Cantrell almost smiled again. "I regretted the loss of my very capable employee at a time when I needed him very much. But I knew the IPO was going ahead, regardless of his threats. So—"

The shrug was an appeal for solidarity. We're men of the world, it said.

"Threats?" asked Hammond.

"He went away so we could change our minds. If we didn't, he claimed he was going to resign and tell the media why."

"And how," Peale asked with deceptive mildness, "were you planning to handle this exposure?"

"By telling the truth. By calling our own media conference and explaining the routine nature of the recoding process."

"On the eve of the road show?" Peale almost squeaked. "What made you think anyone would believe you?"

"The possibility that they wouldn't never crossed my mind."

Or Morse's, from the look of him.

Drew thought he knew the answer, but he asked anyway. "Didn't the technicians notice that the mice were in trouble?"

"Surely that's neither here nor there," Cantrell huffed.

Hammond could have smacked him. "Wade. Larry. Two men are dead. Answer the question."

"Conrad noticed," said Morse. "I noticed. Once we noticed we started recoding."

"Which is why," Cantrell amplified, "I said it was neither here nor there. First of all, if recoding implied anything truly alarming, Conrad would never have mentioned it to David in the first place. And David, I hasten to add, was the only one he did mention it to. Conrad has been with Larry from the beginning. His loyalty is absolute. I hope you're hearing me, gentlemen. No one knows about the recoding except the people in this room and one exceptionally loyal employee."

Hammond's laugh was harsh. "So all's well for the IPO. David's silenced and so is Nat. What a relief. Let's hit the road and sell this stock big."

Peale, decision made, seemed to grow in his chair. "I'm out. The last product was good for eight months on mice. The recoded version would have to work for eight months on people before I'd recommend an underwriting."

"That's preposterous," Cantrell sputtered. "Everyone goes public before human trials. Everyone. Where do you think they get the money for them?"

"Sorry. A stock issue that includes a murdered CFO and a major investor's suicide doesn't strike me as viable."

Ever since Pen's call, Harriman Fraker had been silent, sunk in private worry. Now he spoke. "I want my money. I want it now."

For Esprit, Drew knew. His foundering computer company. Nice that Fraker was in deep financial trouble.

"Of course you want your money," said Cantrell. "And there's no reason why you shouldn't have it. No one needs to connect Nat's unfortunate act with Dynagen."

Drew bit back a powerful urge to taunt Fraker with Esprit. "Correction. I need to."

"What say, Wink?" Hammond asked his surviving partner.

"Ditch the IPO, make a clean breast. Admit we gave Nat too long a leash and let him run wild."

"All right with you, Nanda?"

She nodded. A second ago, something had fallen into place. Nat had accepted the Paladin term sheet without debate because he hoped to avoid Drew, by then identified as Pen's cousin and David's friend. It was their first real clue, and she'd missed it completely. The first clue they'd spotted, of course, was the import of what David had scribbled on Irene Egan's envelope. Crazy Irene, supplier of hard evidence. Next came the clue Nanda herself had generated by leaving her pocketbook in an unlocked drawer, easy pickings for Nat when she was in the bathroom or one of the other partners' offices.

If she didn't love Drew already, she'd have to after this came to light. She was bawling her head off—stupid! How could she have been so stupid!—and refusing to be comforted. So Drew did something wonderful. He opened her pocketbook and took her keys, including the ones, now useless, that Nat had speedily duplicated and returned without her slightest suspicion. Almost ceremoniously, he washed them in hot soapy water, dried them carefully with a towel, and put them back. "I hate it," he then said, "that Nat touched anything of yours."

A man like that, you have to stop crying and be as dear and loving as he is. You have to at least try. Staying stuck in your misery, shamed by your stupidity, is selfishness. And selfishness is the opposite of love.

"Very well," Hammond said. "The IPO is canceled. No, Wade, let me finish. It's time to talk about damage control. Harriman, you want your money now. If you intend to sell your interest to another investor, I trust you'll remember that Hammond, Halsey has approval privileges."

Fraker's long mouth thinned ominously.

"I myself am not inclined to sell," Hammond continued. "I still think we can help Dynagen become a strong company. We have a product aimed at a terrible disease. That means we have value. In the weeks ahead, we'll have to figure out the best way to convert that value to return on investment."

Cantrell wasn't having any. "What about my return on investment? My time and talent? What about Larry's? We didn't tell Nat to kill David. Why should we be hung for it?"

"You're hung," said Drew, "for the same reason you'd be hung if David had come back to blow the whistle. Your IPO's a fraud."

The doctors were still yelling when Pen came into the room. His shirt had been scissored off at the right elbow, revealing a thickly bandaged forearm and hand. Smaller bandages wrapped his left thumb and index finger.

"Geoff's okay," he told Nanda. "Couple of scratches. Wants you to call him when you get home."

After Drew introduced him, Pen began to tell them what they were waiting to hear.

"Partridge found the papers he was looking for and said he had to make a phone call. Highly personal. Would we kindly remove ourselves. I said we were much too interested in his personal life to miss any part of it. Finally we made a deal. We could listen, but we had to sit outside the door. A strange request, but it's been a strange couple of days.

"He got through and asked if that was Clayton. Apparently it was, because he identified himself and launched right in."

"Richardson's big brother," said Drew. "The Marine. The Agent Orange victim."

"Right. Partridge lets him have it right between the eyes. Tells him Dan and his wife got themselves in trouble while he, Clayton, was in Vietnam. The abortionist they went to botched the job and she was hemorrhaging. Just in time, Partridge got her to a real doctor and paid for everything. She survived, but the abortion finished her chances for having children. Not Agent Orange—the abortion."

Pen looked around the table. Except for Nanda and Drew,

no one seemed to be registering the import of this final act. "So there it was—how Partridge got Richardson to kill for him. You do it, he must've said, or I'll tell on you.

"A real old-timey story, huh? Kid brother terrified of big brother's revenge? I mean, here's all this high tech high finance biotech—Geoff and I were sitting there, mulling the ironies, when we heard the crash. Partridge had thrown his desk chair through the window and was going out after it. We were too late to grab him."

There was nothing left to say or do or hear. Drew suggested they adjourn.

"Before we break up," said Cantrell, "I want to assure the investors that Larry and I will continue to exert ourselves to the utmost. We will do what we promised—bring MS-alpha to the market."

Peale said he hoped Cantrell meant the marketplace in general, not the immediate IPO market.

"Exactly, Chris. Though of course we're open to your ideas for an IPO down the road."

Fraker barked smoke. "I have an idea. Find yourselves a reputable finance guy, pronto. Someone who can handle problems like a man, not a scared schoolgirl."

A gnat. Pen didn't even bother to swat it away.

Fraker stood and glared impartially around the table. "I'm off. Meeting my lawyer for lunch."

Ah, thought Drew. Lawyers. *Après le déluge, les avocats.*

Cantrell and Morse rose next. Halfway out, Cantrell sent a parting shot. "The public has a very short memory. We must bear this in mind while we develop new strategies."

No one said a word.

Hammond waited until he heard the door close. "Typical entrepreneur," he said with a wan smile. "Won't take no for an answer."

Chapter 36

Climbing out of the shower the following Sunday morning, Drew smelled corn muffins. Nanda's surprise. Geoff's wife, Patsy, had given her a baking lesson while she was in Newton. The central theory, as Nanda now understood it, was to use stone-ground flours and mix with a light hand. Except for the eggs, which you beat the socks off.

His mouth full, Drew told her they were perfect.

"As good as Sally's?"

"Better. Will you teach me to make them too?"

"Never."

"Why not?"

"A woman gives a man a muffin, she makes him her slave. She teaches him to make his own muffins, she sets him free."

"You shock me, Nanda."

"Admit it. Your expressed desire to bake is totally kneejerk Equal Opportunity. Patently pro forma."

His laugh admitted it. "Still. You really want a slave?"

She smiled comfortably. "Wait'll you try my raisin brans."

He was scanning the business page of the *Times* and finishing his third muffin when a story caught his eye. "Listen to this. A burned stockholder has successfully sued the underwriters of an IPO. Periferex—they make computer peripherals. Used to make. Four months after the issue, spunky little Periferex went belly-up. The court ruled that the prospectus was misleading and full of significant omissions. Stockholders get their money back and court costs."

"Ho. Sounds like Chris Peale has had a narrow escape."

"You guys going for a licensing agreement on MS-alpha?"

"I think so. Charlie's been talking to Hoffman LaRoche. Or

167

is that confidential? Shit. How're we supposed to talk to each other?"

"We'll work it out."

"I didn't notice before, because everything was David. But now that the hum and drum have subsided—"

Drew reached for her hand and kissed its palm. The hum and the drum. Winnie, the theatrical Ninny, was always telling people she loved excitement, bright lights, the hum and the drum.

Subsided, though? There were still reverberations. As Sam Pardee put it, Partridge had died as he lived, leaving the mess to others. With Dynagen on hold, Pen's inheritance from David was just enough to keep David's mother supported with a bit left over. The cousins would split the cost of Alton Amy's wheelchair. The *Becky T.* was for sale.

With difficulty, Pen was facing up to some hard truths about David. Almost surely, he had fled to Maine because he'd been afraid that Cantrell and Morse would wear him down, erode his principled position until he was left with nowhere to stand. He was, in short, his father's son still, a man doomed to obey the demands of others.

Richardson was in jail in Maine, waiting trial. To get him there, Pen had told all to the Boston police right after Partridge's suicide. There'd been some fuss about procedure, anonymous tips, vengeful beatings on Back Bay sidewalks, but nothing Pen hadn't been able to talk himself out of. Richardson was, after all, Maine's problem. And Pen, after all, had learned his lesson. Amateurs should never, under any circumstances, meddle in crime. That's what the police are for, yes sir, no question about it.

In jail Richardson would be safe from Clayton. And Clayton would be safe from making more trouble for himself and his wife than they already had.

After Pen told Nanda and Drew that the *Betty Ann* had been named after Clayton's wife, all three decided that they'd had enough. Nothing wrong with a couple of loose ends left flapping. There's a limit to what the human spirit can bear.

Then, last night, Pen had called, catching them in bed. Could they stand one last horror story? Not really, Drew said, but go ahead.

"Guy I know staffs one of the gay hotlines. The kid who trashed your place called him. Kid's a mass of guilt. Feels terrible about destroying what he kept calling 'helpless beauty.' Yeah, I liked that too. Kid also feels terrible because he's happy Partridge is dead and he's sure that's a sin. Seems he used to babysit Partridge's boys, and one of the boys told his father how they played with their weenies in the bathtub."

Nanda, lying naked beside Drew, saw every shiver of his reaction. When he hung up, she made him tell.

He told. Then, blurting it, "Partridge used people's dirty secrets. Exactly what I did with Willow Barns."

"Are you crazy? There's no comparison. None whatsoever."

"No?"

"Granted you used Willow. Did you pay her dentist so you could? Have you been biding your time ever since? Well then."

"I hated using her. And hurting Arthur Sprague."

"Good. For you, they were fairly hateful things to do. But to make a parallel with Partridge—that's nuts. Plumb loco."

He burrowed against her, breathing her healthy smell.

"Look on the good side," she said. "Pen called after we made love. Not before. Not during."

"Let's get married. Soon as we can."

With his lips in the sweet curve between her neck and shoulder, his proposal was somewhat muffled. But by the way she said, oh yes, let's, he knew she'd heard and taken into herself the full measure of his hopes and desires.

About the Author

Margaret Logan lives in Boston and, when she is not writing, teaches at the Harvard University extension school. She has published a travel memoir, HAPPY ENDINGS.